The Strange Encou...
Sally Shakespeare and Toby Tinker

by

Adam Rawlins

Sally Shakespeare is the bee's knees, smart and popular; Toby Tinker is the opposite, silly and friendless, the class fool.

Usually so sensible, Sally believes that her stories come true if read aloud, and perhaps they do. When Toby disappears, Sally blames herself and decides to take action, even if it means defying everyone who cares for her.

An intriguing story of fear and friendship for readers aged 10 and over.

For
Lucy and Arno

**The Strange Encounter of
Sally Shakespeare and Toby Tinker**

Text copyright©2013 Adam Rawlins
Cover Design©2013 Sarah Hughes
Edited by Vanessa Hinds

ISBN 978-1-908577-40-5

First Published 2013

Hawkwood Books 2013

We all have a fear of the unknown; what one does with that fear will make all the difference in the world.

Lillian Russell

If we let things terrify us, life will not be worth living.

Seneca

Aloud

Everyone laughed at Toby Tinker who never did anything right, even Sally Shakespeare who never did anything wrong. When Sally received the usual compliments from any of her teachers, she blushed with pride whilst Toby made rude sounds from the back of the class where he lived in his own, private universe. Sally ignored him, as everyone tried to do, only hoping that *it* wouldn't happen again and spoil everything.

'*It*' was what happened when her amazing stories were read aloud, which is why she panicked when Mr Jarvis, their Year 7 English teacher, said he wanted to read her latest masterpiece to the class.

Drat and double drat.

"Oh no, sir. Please, you mustn't!"

Sally looked horrified but Mr Jarvis misunderstood; he thought she was just being modest.

"Nothing to be shy about, Sally. It'll go down a

treat, believe me. Perhaps you'd like to read it yourself?"

She didn't want it read aloud by anyone.

"I'll read it!" said Toby Tinker, and everyone laughed because they all knew that Toby couldn't read, or write for that matter. He couldn't do anything except be the class fool.

Mr Jarvis opened the exercise book at Sally's story and, despite her protest, started to read. Sally stared at the floor, apparently waiting for it to open and swallow her, never to be seen again.

"Remember what I asked you to do," he said to the class. "The story was called 'The Beast'. Sally wrote about a school terrorised by a mysterious creature. This is how it begins:

'Deep in the heart of the school, the beast awoke. Its red eyes shone like fiery coals and its black silky skin rippled like waves in a dark sea.'"

It only took a few of Sally's words to make even the most doubting of Thomas's in the class sit up and pay attention. Sally seemed to know every word in the dictionary, and a few more besides. She also managed to put them together in just the right way. Even Toby perked up and stopped his silliness for a while.

"'It stood and stretched, flexing its powerful muscles. It was hungry and needed food. Here in the boiler room there was nothing, just warmth and quiet, whilst from above drifted the sounds of fresh meat, walking and talking. The beast dribbled on the dusty floor, prowling, fiery-eyed, ravenous.

'From its belly came a soft, threatening growl, full of menace. Food! It must have food!

'The beast knew how to hunt. It needed darkness and so it moved through the inside of the building until it found the blackest of black places and hid, patiently, silently. When the door of the dark place opened, the beast licked its lips, bared its claws, waited not a second too long... and pounced!

'That was the last the school saw of its doomed caretaker.'"

The story continued and Mr Jarvis read it to an enthralled audience. When he had finished, he took a deep breath and said, "Well done Sally, amazing stuff. And you see, nothing terrible happened."

Sally whispered, "No sir," unconvinced.

Toby stared at her, his look giving away nothing, a perfect mask, perhaps hiding envy, perhaps fear or even wonder, it was impossible to tell.

Mr Jarvis set the children an exercise and they began in their usual, desperately slow way, aware that they couldn't match Shakespeare, neither William nor Sally. Some of them seemed to have a real block against getting started with anything, as if learning was the worst thing ever invented, but the one who found it hardest of all was Toby Tinker.

Toby was staring at the silver locket in which he kept a picture of his grandmother. He always wore it around his neck and gazed at it whenever he was feeling agitated. Like now.

He felt something stab his side and turned to see Jonas Hayes, a sour and dangerous boy, smirking at him.

"Let's see your story," said Jonas.

Toby didn't know how to deal with Jonas. He'd tried being friendly, but that didn't work, and it wasn't in his nature to be tough. He showed his story to Jonas, two pages written in thick black pencil, totally unreadable. The story might have been wonderful if he could have got the stuff in his head onto the page, but something always happened to it as the ideas trickled down his arm into the pencil and onto paper; they got muddled and lost. He tried to read it but couldn't understand his own handwriting. Jonas and his bully-boy friends laughed and knocked the book onto the floor. They all knew that Toby's work was rubbish. The teachers gave his condition a name that sounded like a terrible disease, but all Toby knew was that he couldn't spell and couldn't write and he was dead jealous of Sally Shakespeare who wrote like the Harry Potter lady and the Chocolate Factory man rolled into one, only she was just eleven years old. It wasn't fair and he was angry about it, as he was about most things.

Half an hour after Sally's effort had blown the class away, there was a commotion as she rushed to Mr Jarvis's desk with the exercise book open.

"Please sir, look what Toby did!"

The story of 'The Beast' had been crossed out with angry black lines, and the pages torn.

"Did you see him do it?"

"Jackie did."

"Jackie, come here." Jackie went there. "Did you

see Toby do this?"

"What, sir?"

"This, Jackie, did you see Toby do it?"

"Well sir, I was sitting doing my work and I looked up and I saw him staring at her book."

"You actually saw him do it?"

"I didn't actually see him do it, but I saw him touch the book, sir."

"Toby, come here."

Toby went there, giggling nervously.

"Did you do this?"

Mr Jarvis showed Toby the marks on Sally's story.

"No, sir."

"Jackie says she saw you touching it."

"I didn't do nuffing, sir."

Mr Jarvis didn't know what to make of Toby. He wanted to help him because he was a kind man and had become a teacher to change the future, but the class wore him out and his patience was often wafer thin. Besides, proving these things was always tricky.

"Toby, did you do it or not?"

"No! No! No! No! No!"

Mr Jarvis opted out of making a decision and decided to foist the whole thing onto the headmaster.

"Go and explain it to Mr Crabshaw, Toby," he said. "Take the book and tell him exactly what happened."

Toby mumbled something to Sally and Jackie.

"What was that?"

Toby muttered, "Nuffing," and went out, slamming the door behind him.

When Mr Jarvis turned back to Sally, she was crying. Jackie had her arm round her but she was clearly distressed.

"We'll get it sorted," said Mr Jarvis. "You can read through the scribble alright. It isn't lost forever."

Sally shook her head. That wasn't the problem.

"Are you afraid of Toby?"

"No, sir!"

"That's good. He doesn't mean any harm, you know. Anything else?"

Sally was very quiet.

"Are you upset that I read your story aloud?"

Sally stood stock still, looking down.

"You're worried about something. I can tell."

"No, sir, really, I'm alright," she lied.

When Mr Jarvis asked the class if anyone knew who'd defaced Sally's story, Jonas said, "It was Sally's beast, sir," trying to say it as a joke, but it didn't sound like a joke at all, which was strange. Jonas Stamp was a hard boy and would probably stare out the devil if it got someone else into trouble. Why should he be worried unless he was guilty? But then, everyone was looking guilty.

"Well, class, someone must know what happened, and why. It's the end of lesson now. If whoever knows wants to stay behind and tell me, I'd appreciate it, otherwise I'll set a detention."

There was a groan from the class, but they were

dismissed and went out in a huff. Mr Jarvis hoped that someone would remain behind but none of them did. Over the next few days, there was a change in the atmosphere. Mr Jarvis was aware of things like that and he knew the children were keeping something from him. He assumed it was the truth about who spoiled Sally's story, and in a way it was, but not the way he thought.

A week passed and other things happened, small things, but wrong things, like thefts and damage and threats and all manner of rumour. A detention was given but achieved nothing. No one owned up and no one was found out.

Nor had Mr Crabshaw got very far with Toby. In fact, he had delegated the whole thing to someone else who had delegated it to someone else, confirming to Toby that the world was full of words, none of which he understood, and empty of meaning.

The tension grew, way beyond what a vindictive little crossing out should have created, and it was with some relief that, at last, Mr Jarvis found out why. Sally and her best friends Michelle and Jackie stayed behind at the end of a lesson.

"Yes?" asked Mr Jarvis.

"Sally wants to tell you something," said Michelle.

"What is it Sally?"

"You won't believe me."

"I might."

"It's happened before."

"What has?"

"Different things. Oh, I don't know how to say it."

Michelle tried to help.

"It's her story, sir, don't you remember?"

"Remember what?"

"She asked you not to read it."

"Well?"

"You did read it," said Michelle.

"So?"

"Sally's got this thing, sir," said Jackie.

"What thing?"

"Well," said Sally, "it doesn't happen all the time. But I have to be careful."

"Are you ill?"

"No, sir."

"But sir, she's not ordinary. It's really weird."

"What is?"

"It's my stories," said Sally, "it's alright if you read them silently. But if you read them aloud, I mean, I know it sounds silly."

"It does a bit," confessed Mr Jarvis, "and I don't see what it's got to do with what's happened."

He had visions of his armchair at home, waiting to be sat in.

"I'm normally very careful," said Sally, "but it was such an interesting story and I wanted to please you and I got carried away."

"So?"

"Don't you see, sir?" asked Michelle.

"No."

"It's her stories," said Jackie, as if Mr Jarvis was being especially thick.

"Yes?"

"If you read them aloud."

"Yes?"

"Like you did," said Michelle.

"Yes? Yes?"

"They come true," said Sally.

Beast

Neither Michelle nor Jackie could remember just when they'd started believing in Sally's special power. But they did. They had it firmly stuck in their heads that whatever Sally wrote, if it was read aloud, came true. The evidence was slim and suspect, but they'd looked for it and seen it many times, and so now they believed in the beast. They'd even managed to scare the rest of the class and put the heebie-jeebies into Jonas Stamp, which was some achievement.

"Mr Jarvis will never believe me," said Sally.

"He might," said Michelle, "but we'll have to prove it."

The question was how. None of the little things they'd witnessed over the past year, ever since they left junior school, would stand up in a court of law, but that didn't matter. Faith was everything. Crumbs, you had millions of people wandering around Planet Earth believing in Gods they could never prove were real. This was no different. They believed the beast existed. It might not have done before Mr Jarvis read the story, but it did now, and the thought frightened them. They didn't know how to prove it though. They needed absolute, incontrovertible evidence, and that was clearly a scary thing to do, as well as rather difficult.

Little things had happened and they ascribed all of them to the beast, things which any Tom, Dick or Harry could have done. But also big and horrible things reported daily on the news, bad stories upon bad stories, the beast was responsible.

"It has come true," said Sally. "I feel it."

Everyone respected Sally. She was a clever girl and generally very sensible, but she had this bee in her bonnet and her friends believed her. After all, who was to say it wasn't true, only adults and teachers, and what did they know except the obvious. None of them believed in anything exciting or different.

"So what shall we do?" asked Jackie.

"Suppose you write another story," suggested Michelle, "where someone kills the beast? Mr Jarvis, for instance. How about that?"

"I can try," said Sally, "but if it's a different story, the beast might not know it's supposed to die. I might make everything worse."

Sally wished she hadn't written the story in the first place. Now everyone would blame her when something really terrible happened, and something terrible was sure to happen, she knew it. As soon as her teacher had read the story, she felt the world shift slightly. She knew that what she'd written wasn't just words, but a spell that would give birth to something fearful and dangerous.

Michelle and Jackie comforted her as they walked around the school grounds trying not to think of beasts and blood, but fearing that blood and beasts were almost certainly unavoidable.

"What do you think it looks like, Sally?" asked Michelle, but Sally didn't want to say, afraid of making matters worse.

"No one saw it. It was just there."

"And it really killed the caretaker?" asked Michelle.

Sally nodded, on the one hand certain that their own caretaker, a kindly, ancient chap, was still alive and kicking, but on the other, knowing that his life was in terrible danger.

"We've got to try and find it," she said. "I don't think it will hurt me, not if it knows that I made it."

"But it would hurt us, wouldn't it?"

"Not if I told it not to," said Sally.

They weren't convinced, but it was her beast so they had to trust her.

"The boiler room," said Sally. "That's where we have to go. Doesn't matter if we get into trouble after, we have to go and see."

Michelle and Jackie were about as keen on the idea as they were of taking a long run off a short pier. Not even the possibility of asking some of their older siblings to come with, or even, heaven forbid, a teacher, gave them courage.

"They wouldn't," said Michelle. "They'd think we're nuts."

"We are nuts," said Jackie. "But that doesn't

mean we're wrong."

"What about telling Crabshaw?"

"The headmaster? You must be joking!"

They discussed various people but no one seemed likely. They were all too sensible to believe in such a cock and bull idea.

"Then we'll have to go alone," said Sally.

They were walking slowly and talking quietly, afraid of where this was leading them.

"Alright," said Michelle. "I'll come with you."

"And me, I suppose," said Jackie.

They thought about this for a few days, working up enough courage to do what had to be done. At lunchtime on the third day, the three of them, checking first for spies, disappeared around the back of the school, over to a flight of stone steps and down to the boiler room door.

"It's bound to be locked," said Jackie.

She and Michelle hoped it would be. This was taking a silly risk. A locked door would be a good excuse to forget the whole plan.

They stood there staring, as if waiting for the door to open by itself. They felt stupid one second, afraid the next. No one wanted to try. They could hear their hearts beat. Noise from the playground on the other side of the building seemed like a long, long way away. This was a foolish and dangerous thing to do. They were sensible girls, so why were they even thinking about it?

Sally did the deed.

She turned the old handle and the heavy iron

door creaked open.

They half expected the beast to rush past them with a roar.

Nothing.

"What now?" asked Jackie.

Sally reached into her bag and took out the torch she'd brought from home.

"I'll go in," she said. "You follow. Close the door behind you."

"Close the door?" said Jackie. "With us inside?"

"It's not locked," said Sally. "And I've got my torch."

They trod carefully and quietly, knowing they were doing wrong but unable to stop themselves. The light from the torch lit up a series of rooms. It was hot, stuffy and uncomfortable. Even with the torchlight, the area was full of menacing shadows.

"Here's a light switch," said Michelle.

"No!" said Sally. "Don't use it. We'll get used to the dark in a moment."

After a few seconds, their eyes accustomed to the dark and they began to see the shapes of huge metal boilers. They could also see chinks of light coming from the holes in the ceiling where pipes passed through to the main school buildings. These chinks gave some lifesaving light to the awful blackness, and they could even see without the torch.

"Now what?" said Jackie. "It's obviously not here. This is daft. Let's go."

"We've only just come in," Sally insisted. "We have to wait a while."

She found a spot by one of the boiler drums with their backs against the wall where they could still see the entrance door. All three sat down, looked around and waited for something which, deep down, they knew would never happen. Stories did not come to life and beasts did not live in school boiler rooms.

And yet, they were scared.

The only sound, apart from their breathing, was the distant noise of children running and shouting in the playground, faint now, like a fading echo.

"It's like they're a hundred miles away," said Sally.

"I wish I was a hundred miles away," said Jackie.

The jumbled noises drifted down as if from another world. The longer they sat, the further away and the more unrecognisable were the sounds that reached them.

"I think," said Sally after a couple of minutes that felt like a couple of years, "that we should go further in. If the beast is here, it wouldn't sit by the entrance would it?"

"It might," said Jackie, not wanting to chance her luck any further. "Let's not do that, Sal. Let's stay here."

But Sally stood up and her friends followed, slowly edging into the adjoining room. As they did so, the echoing sounds from above diminished and died, and so did the little light from the main entrance door.

"Remember which way we came," said Michelle,

"just in case we have to get out in a hurry."

"Over here," said Sally. "Come on."

She found a spot similar to the first, but deeper into the second room, darker and quieter.

"This isn't clever," Jackie whispered. "I'm scared, Sal."

Jackie and Michelle were equally scared, but they bravely, or foolishly, followed their friend because they trusted and respected her. She was the brightest of all of them and they trusted her, even beyond their own better judgement.

They sat themselves down, backs against the wall again, and waited. Shadows in the gloom took on strange forms and became, in their imagination, all things except that which they truly were.

Sally opened her bag, hunted around inside and took out...

"Cat food?" Michelle whispered. "Cat food, Sal?"

"Bait," Sally explained.

She had brought a tin opener and a plastic spoon and after quietly opening the tin, placed the lump of brown splodgy gunge in a bowl and placed it close to the third room.

"Is this a real beast or a giant cat we're looking for?" Michelle asked.

Sally didn't think the question worth an answer. She hunkered down again and waited a few minutes.

Nothing.

"I think we should go into the next room," she said. "The deeper in, the more likely we are to see it."

"No way!" said Jackie.

"Likewise," said Michelle. "Sorry Sal, this is far enough."

Sounds took on new meaning in the tangible gloom. It was the easiest thing in the world to imagine that anything they heard was the horrid breathing of a skulking creature.

"I can't see the cat food," whispered Sally.

"I can," said Michelle. "It's still there."

Actually, she couldn't see it, but she didn't want Sally wandering off on her own and leaving them.

They waited, feeling a combination of anxiety and fear. A moment more and Sally would call it a day, but something happened.

A noise, different from the almost inaudible far away school noises, much closer.

"What was that?" asked Jackie, terrified.

"It's coming!" said Michelle. "Look!"

From the depths of the third room they saw a moving shadow whose outline melted indistinctly into the darkness. With it came noises which, to the frightened girls, seemed like great snorts and monstrous scratchings.

"Let's go, Sal!" whispered Jackie.

But Sally, possessed by some stubborn streak of bravado, stood up and said aloud, "Beast, beast, this is Sally Shakespeare. I made you. You know me. We're here."

"Sally!" whispered Jackie, astonished. "What are you doing?"

"Sssh!" whispered Sally,

As if it had been switched off by some unseen hand, the noise ceased and the quiet of the boiler room returned.

"Let's go, now," said Jackie. "Please!"

"Yes, we must," said Michelle.

Sally sighed, then said, "Alright, I'll just have one last look..."

"Don't!" hissed Jackie, but Sally was on her way.

When she came back, her face was full of animation, something between excitement and fear.

"What's the matter?" asked Michelle.

Sally showed them the bowl.

It was empty.

They stared at it as if it was the one ring or the holy grail or a horcrux, or perhaps all of them rolled into one. An empty, plastic cat food bowl.

"It must have been hungry," said Sally. "That was a whole tin! And we didn't see a thing."

"Maybe it's invisible!" said Jackie, looking around in even greater fear, half expecting to be grabbed by an invisible demon.

They hurried to the door, opened it, only to be faced by a different type of beast.

Hiding their eyes from the sudden bright light, they peered up to the top of the stairs where two great figures stood like sentinels. One was the school caretaker, and the other was their headmaster, Mr. Wilfred S. Crabshaw.

"What the...?"

The next few minutes were the most excruciating of their lives. They received a grilling that would have melted metal. Their ears burned and their stomachs churned, wave after wave of angry chastisement from a fearsome man in a fearsome mood.

"Those tanks are red hot! You could have been killed in there! What the devil were you doing, skulking around in the dark? Have you lost your senses, girls?"

And so on for a full ten minutes.

But at least they were still alive.

That was no small thing. Mr Jarvis, once he'd got to hear about their foolishness, reminded them of how dangerous the world was and how much care you had to take, every day, to stay alive and kicking.

"I didn't want to scare the beast, sir," said Sally who was almost crying again. She hadn't cried when the headmaster had shouted, but she cried now her favourite teacher was telling her off, and being shouted at by someone you liked could be the worst thing in the world, at least until the next worst thing turned up.

"I hope you are upset," said Mr Jarvis feeling a hard to bear mixture of anger and pity. "Your lives are more important than anything else. I'm so disappointed with you all."

"But, sir," said Michelle. "No one believed us. We had to prove it."

"Prove what, Michelle? That a beast lives in our boiler room? Have you been eating magic mushrooms or something?"

They had no idea what these were, but they got the meaning.

"It was there, sir! It ate the food!" said Sally.

She told Mr Jarvis the story of the cat food, but he wasn't interested. The caretaker had a cat, and if it wasn't that, it could have been a stray mouse or grateful rat, but not a stupid, silly fantasy of a beast. It was madness and he made them promise, as the head had done, never to do it again.

Punishments and verbal torture over, never to be forgotten, they were relieved to get home, eat, sleep and forget the whole silliness of it all. The weekend lay ahead. Monday was the beginning of a new week and they could make a brand new start.

Cornered

Toby loved the story of the beast. He hadn't meant it when he said it was rubbish. He was jealous, but although he knew deep down that it was wrong to feel like that, he didn't know what to do about it. He didn't know what to do about most things that happened to him and solved the problem by playing the fool so that people would notice him. If they didn't notice him then another kind of beast would start mocking him and make him feel bad about himself. So he acted the fool that day, pretending to be a monster, crouching down, jumping up in the air and swinging his arms around like a wild thing. "Roooarr!" he yelled. Some younger children saw him and didn't know whether to laugh or be afraid. When he charged at them they just ran off screaming.

Toby didn't understand where the anger inside him came from. It came and went like a hurricane, without warning and without control. He felt it might not come if he could just get some things straight in his head, but he wasn't sure what or how. No one seemed able to tell him, either. No one. He ran around in circles shouting his favourite word

"Boo!" but even this didn't make the feelings inside him go away, the feelings of great loneliness and fear.

Jonas Stamp and friends didn't help. In fact they made it worse, picking on him whenever they felt like it.

"Hey, look at Nutter!"

Toby ran towards the boys jumping and screaming. They couldn't touch him if he pretended to be someone or something else. Or that was what he thought, but when Toby was close enough, Jonas punched him on the nose.

"You're an idiot," said Jonas.

Toby started crying. When he cried, the sobs came from deep inside, like almost everything else about him, uncontrollable. He stood there with great lumpy tears rolling down his face. They couldn't enter his world, these bully boys, they couldn't even leave him alone in it. They spoiled everything. Everything!

Toby ran off around the back of the school and tried to dry his eyes. He was so miserable, he felt nothing could lift his unhappiness, but he saw a peculiar sight - that clever clogs girl Sally Shakespeare and her friends disappearing down the steps to the boiler room! His head was full of pictures again. He waited and watched, expecting to hear screams from the lair of the beast. When the school keeper turned up, saw the open door and called the headmaster, Toby expected them to carry out what was left of the girls after the beast had eaten them, but they walked out untouched, just a bit shamefaced.

What kind of a beast was it that didn't kill little girls?

"Boo!" he shouted, and ran off, desperate for school to end.

Not that home was much better. Toby's mum and dad were heavy handed. They tried to solve all problems by shouting and threatening, but there were too many problems and in the end none of them got solved that way.

That night, they were in a horrible mood and Toby kept to his room. He lay on his unmade bed looking at some tatty old books he had stolen from various places. Well, he couldn't afford them, and his mum and dad wouldn't buy him one in a month of Sundays, so he didn't feel bad about it. What did anyone expect? There was one which had been properly borrowed from the public library, but that was two years ago. He flicked through them for a while, wondering what they were about and wishing he could read, but he couldn't. He asked himself what was the point of school if it made him unhappy and he couldn't read or write a word. There wasn't an answer.

Eventually, he grew sleepy, threw all the rubbish off his bed and climbed in.

He might have dropped off to sleep straight away, but he began to hear the familiar screaming and shouting from his mum and dad's room. They were arguing again. Toby couldn't make out what was being said, but he started silently mocking them while looking at his reflection in a broken mirror. It was like a puppet show and it made him laugh to see his own face imitating his parents. He heard his own name mentioned a few times but couldn't make out what was said about him. Probably nothing good.

He was awake now. It was past one in the morning and he didn't feel like going back to bed. Instead, an idea popped into his head. He wasn't sure where it came from and he didn't care. It was a good idea. He dressed, took up his bag, threw some clothes and a torch into it, pinched a few things from the fridge and slipped out the front door.

He had always felt like a cornered animal, hunted down with nowhere to run. His mum and dad blew hot and cold, mostly cold, and even if they blew hot, they didn't know what was wrong with him nor bothered to put it right. At school, if he tried to learn, Jonas Stamp or some other bully would have a go at him. It hadn't been too bad in the juniors, but now it was worse than he'd imagined. He waited for an adult, somewhere, to see inside his head and sort him out, to free him. But no one came. This little adventure at night was the freest he'd been for ages, maybe for ever.

It was October and already the nights were colder and less friendly than summer. There was a chill, and the autumn winds had begun the long freezing of this part of Earth. Toby walked past the school which appeared ghostly in the orangey glow of the streetlights. He pulled a face and stuck his tongue, once for Jonas Stamp, once for the teachers and once for...

He froze before he could stick out his tongue again. Something was happening that shouldn't be happening, near the school gate. He couldn't see clearly but there was definitely something going on. He made a slight movement and knocked a tin can which rolled away. The noise sounded like thunder in the still of the night. He felt unseen eyes pinning him down, cornering him, just like everyone and everything else seemed to corner him.

Move!

He raced away, as fast and far as he could, then hid.

He stood still as a statue and listened.

Nothing.

The longer he waited, the safer he felt. How much time had passed? A minute? An hour?

After a while, he came out and looked cautiously around. It seemed safe.

He wondered what it was that he'd seen. If it had been the beast, it had looked remarkably human, perhaps like someone he knew, a different kind of beast but not the bizarre, wild creature that haunts nightmares. This was a familiar sort of fright.

Foolishly, although he couldn't seem to help himself, he decided to go back and have another look. He threaded his way along the deserted streets, always checking to be sure the coast was clear, until he found himself close to the perimeter fence. If he poked his head around the corner, he could see it, about fifty yards away.

No one and nothing.

Except...

Something was different.

Toby moved closer, dodging behind lamp posts, his eyes widening as he saw what had been done, and what all the school would see, in just a few hours.

Don't!

Sally was furious with Toby Tinker. It was his fault she'd got into trouble. She'd written the story, but Toby was the beast. Why couldn't he be normal like everyone else! Why couldn't he just disappear altogether! She felt guilty, but she couldn't help it; Toby Tinker was trouble. He shouldn't be in their school at all!

As soon as she thought the thoughts, Sally said to herself, 'Don't!' because she knew they were wrong, but she'd had much worse thoughts when she was being scolded, and as much as she tried to forget it, it kept coming back.

"You alright Sally?" he mother asked. "You look a bit put out."

"I'm okay."

Sally sat in the kitchen while her mum made tea.

"Everything alright at school?"

Sally said, "Mum? Supposing you've done something which isn't really your fault but it's still you that's done it. I mean you didn't do it on purpose, but it happened and it's you that made it happen. What would you do?"

"I'm not sure I know what you mean, Sally.

Sounds awfully complicated. Is it a bad thing?"

"I don't know. I hope not."

"Well, if it's not your fault... can it be put right?"

"I don't know that either."

"Are you in trouble, darling?"

"No."

"Do you want me to talk to the teachers?"

"It's just 'suppose', mum. Suppose no one believes you when you tell them something."

"What are they being told?"

"Doesn't matter what; they just don't."

"Perhaps it's not being told to them properly."

"It was."

"Are you sure it's the truth?"

"I think so."

"But you're not one hundred per cent positive?"

Sally couldn't answer. She wanted to tell her mum that she had a special power, that things she wrote came true, but when she said it, it sounded stupid. When it was stuck in her head, it was perfectly believable, but as soon as she opened her mouth to talk about it, it changed.

"Don't stick to things just out of stubbornness Sally," said her mother. "We're a stubborn family, you know, but it's not always the right way to be. It all depends. If you are absolutely sure you're right then that's different, you have to stick to what you believe, but if you're wrong, just let go."

"But if you can't prove it?"

"Well, what you believe is important. If you believe something, that should be good enough. If you're right, that's wonderful. But if in the end you're wrong, you have to own up and say so. It's not the end of the world. Good friends will stick by you."

Sally hoped this was true.

"Of course," her mum continued, "it's no use believing black is white and white is black. Some things are daft to believe, full stop."

Sally decided that the rules of life were too complicated. One minute her mum told her something that she liked and made her happy, the next she told her something annoying that made her uncomfortable again. Why couldn't there be a simple answer to everything?

She did her gym and music. She went out with different friends and forgot Toby and the beast and an empty bowl. A new week began and she went to school certain that everything would be fine, only to see crowds gathered around a gaping hole in the school fence.

Sally knew at once what had happened. Her beast had chewed up the fence, and probably Toby along with it. What on Earth would she say when the police asked her terrible questions? She would be locked up as a witch or something!

It turned out that the school had been broken into. Someone, or something thought Sally, had broken in, or broken out thought Sally again, and stolen – well, very little. No damage had been done and not much had been taken, although the thieves had known where to go to find money. Fortunately for the school, unfortunately for the thieves, there'd been no money to steal. But as the day went on, rumours grew, especially that something was indeed missing, and that something was Toby Tinker.

His parents had apparently reported him missing over the weekend, and he hadn't reappeared on Monday. The police at first thought that he was somehow involved with the robbery, and they hadn't dismissed the idea, not completely. But they were stumped. And so was everyone else.

Sally's reassurance after talking with her mother vanished in a puff of doubt. The hole in the fence and Toby missing were obvious pieces of evidence that she'd been right all along. No one believed her, not even her mother, but Sally was no one's fool.

She thought the police would track her down in some clever television detective type way, but this didn't happen. They didn't even talk to her, not Monday nor Tuesday, although Mr Jarvis talked to all of them on Wednesday.

"As you know," he said, "Toby hasn't been in school for a few days. He's also been missing from home."

"Is he dead, sir?" asked Jonas Stamp, smirking.

"Jonas, try not to be so childish. You've all seen the police here. They've been talking to the headmaster and they're coming in here tomorrow morning. We're going to send a letter out to your parents to tell them what's happened and if necessary they'll be invited to talk to the police over the weekend. Hopefully Toby will turn up before then, safe and sound."

"What happened, sir?"

"That's what the police have come to find out. Try not to be upset, I'm sure everything will be alright."

Mr Jarvis tried to sound reassuring, but was upset himself.

"Sir?"

Jonas again.

"Did the beast get him?"

Some of the class sniggered but Sally's stomach churned. She must have been as white as a ghost, she felt so faint. She'd wished him gone and he'd gone! She'd thought it and hoped for it and now it had happened! How could she deny this was her fault?

"Don't be cruel, Jonas."

Cruel. Sally thought that it wasn't Jonas Stamp who was the cruel one in the class; she, Sally Shakespeare, was the bad girl, a really bad girl who did terrible things just by thinking about them. Her thoughts came back to haunt her. She remembered how angry she'd been, how fed up she was because Toby had defaced her story. She remembered the words that had come to her and that she'd tried to put out of her mind but couldn't because she was so furious. They came back to her now, horribly real.

"I wish he was dead!"

Easy

At break, after dismissing a particularly difficult Year Ten English class, Mr Jarvis was lost in thoughts of his own when Sally approached him to say, "Sir, I know what's happened to Toby."

"You do? Explain."

"He's dead, sir."

Mr Jarvis was fairly pale skinned at the best of times, but he turned a whiter shade of pale.

"How do you know that, Sally?"

"I just know."

"That's not an answer Sally. It's a very serious thing you're saying, the most serious thing you could say. Now, how do you know that?"

Mr Jarvis sensed what was coming next.

"I was angry with him and I said to myself, 'I wish Toby Tinker was dead' then he went missing."

"Sally..."

"I'm not sure how, sir, but it's true. I think my beast must have got him."

"Oh, Sally, really!"

"Don't you believe me?"

"I believe you believe it, but no I don't believe you're right! Of course not! No one will."

"Why not?"

Mr Jarvis was a thoughtful man whose contemplations about life were too often interrupted by the inescapable noise of classroom life, but now that he had a serious discussion on his hands, he didn't know what to say. It was serious, yes, but also ridiculous.

"Because things like that just don't happen, Sally. Things don't come true because we write about them or say them."

"They do for me."

"Why for you?"

"Because they do. Sometimes, anyway."

"No, Sally, they don't. It might seem as if they do but it's just coincidence. Life is full of coincidence. You know what that is?"

"Not really."

"When two things happen together that seem connected, but they aren't at all."

"How do you know?"

"Know what?"

"That they're not connected."

"Because common sense tells me so. Life is full of… activity. Some time or other there's going to be coincidences when they seem to be connected, but they're not at all."

"Like what?"

"Like your beast, for example. Just because you wrote about one doesn't mean that it's here."

"Who did all the other things every time I wrote a story?"

"What other things, Sally?"

Sally and her friends knew about 'the other things', but Mr Jarvis didn't. They'd concocted a whole raft of spurious events to prove the point, but Sally had a feeling that if she reeled them off to a sensible man like Mr Jarvis, they would sound silly.

"Well?" he asked, seeing her searching for evidence of her crazy idea.

"I know it sounds ridiculous sir, I do, but they happened at the time and I just felt they were my fault. I felt it!"

"Sally, Sally, Sally!"

Mr Jarvis would have laughed if the situation allowed it, but Toby was missing and anything could have happened. He didn't feel like laughing.

"Look," he said, "strange things happen in life, it's what you make of it all. People believe all kinds of nonsense. If it makes them happy and does no harm, then that's okay. But you can't blame yourself for something as serious as this."

Sally asked him, "Who made that hole in the fence and broke the door down, sir?"

"If I knew, Sally, I'd tell the police. But it wasn't a beast."

Sally looked glum. She just didn't know what to believe or what was the truth. In a way she wanted to believe Mr Jarvis but she wasn't ready yet to put aside what seemed so obvious to her.

"If he's really dead," she said, "it'll be my fault."

"No it won't, and you mustn't say it! He's missing, that's all, and missing children can turn up again any time. I'll tell you something I shouldn't, because you probably know it already, that Toby is a very difficult pupil to teach. He has what we call learning and emotional difficulties. He wants everything and wants it now and he gets frustrated because things aren't the way they should be for him. I got angry too sometimes and wished he'd not come to school, but I don't take the blame for what's happened. And neither must you. You understand?"

"Only a bit, sir."

"If you've got anything important to tell the police, you make sure you tell them, but don't tell them things like that or they won't listen to anything at all. It'll seem to them like the boy, or rather the girl, who cried wolf. You know what I mean?"

She nodded.

"Good. Now go and clear your head and try to make up with some of your friends. I think they're keeping away from you because you've told them all this stuff and nonsense and got them into trouble."

Over the next couple of days, Sally tried to do this, but it wasn't easy. Lots of ideas were still bothering her and, most important, Toby was still missing. She was wandering lonely as a cloud in a spot where her friends would usually have joined her, but since the boiler room fiasco, they'd kept a distance. She sat down on a bench, swinging her legs backwards and forwards, thinking hard about the turn events had taken but not making much sense of them.

"You alright?"

Michelle stood there, rather warily. Sometimes Michelle looked like a teenager, sometimes she looked like a little girl again. Sally always felt too young, as if she was never going to grow up.

After a few awkward moments, Michelle sat down next to her and said, "Friends?"

"You know we are."

Michelle couldn't make her mind up whether Sally Shakespeare was a genius, a witch or just good at telling stories. They'd known each other since Year 1 and were best friends, but even best friends have tricky times together and this was one of them. Jackie would have joined them but she was off sick that day, and besides, her parents had warned her about getting into trouble again with 'that egghead' Sally Shakespeare.

The little adventure in the boiler rooms had put a strain on their friendship. Friends were supposed to support and trust each other but Michelle and Jackie had lost a little trust in their brainy leader. Despite trying to keep it secret, everyone seemed to know what had happened. Some had even challenged Sally asking her if she was the one who made the beast that killed Toby. It all sounded tremendously silly, but there was a horrible fear inside Sally which, despite everything, seemed to whisper that they might be right.

Everyone was worried, and rightly so. A boy had disappeared and the rumour was that some kind of monster had killed him. None of them knew anything about the world and so they believed the first thing they were told. All fingers pointed at the clever girl from Year 7, Sally Shakespeare, the one who had made it all happen. What they didn't understand was why she was still free and not in prison. They probably thought she had the beast under some kind of control and could make it do what she wanted. And if she didn't like someone... no, she mustn't think like that. But she was puzzled. Here she was trying her best at school to work hard and do well and this terrible thing had been landed on her from nowhere, all because of a stupid story. It was unfair.

"Penny for your thoughts?" Michelle said.

"Not worth it," said Sally. "And anyway, you know what I'm thinking about."

A few other Year Seven children had gathered into a group nearby and were staring at the two girls.

"What's your problem?" Michelle said.

"You're the one that made the beast."

"What are you on about? There's no beast."

"Everyone says there is."

"Like who?"

"Everyone. And they say something else too."

"What else?"

"That it killed Toby because he started on you."

Sally was glad that Michelle was there. She wouldn't have liked to deal with this alone. She didn't know what to say. It was like these kids had read her mind and were telling her what she was most afraid of being true. How could that have happened? She denied it, but the denial sounded hollow. She grew angry, but only because she was nervous.

"That's right," said Michelle, "and if you bother us any more, it'll bite your silly head off. Now get lost! Dumb and dumber," Michelle whispered to Sally as the wary group wandered off. "Take no notice."

"But I believe it too," said Sally. "Maybe I did do it."

She told Michelle what she'd said to their English teacher and what he'd said to her, that things didn't happen because you wrote about them.

"He's right, Sal."

"Maybe. Maybe not."

"A real beast would have shown itself by now," said Michelle. "What's it afraid of? Not us?"

"If it was there," said Sally pointing vaguely to the boiler room, it's probably gone now. What if it really has got Toby, what can I do?"

Michelle was in a bit of a fix herself. Her parents, like Jackie's, had warned her off foolish adventures, but she saw how upset Sally still was and said, "Why don't you try what we said the other day? Write another story killing the beast and letting Toby go free and making it end happy."

This sounded like the best and safest chance to put things right so, after school, they set to work.

"*The wild beast roamed the corridors...*" suggested Michelle.

"No, that's too dangerous," said Sally. "Let's start with Toby. '*Toby lay tired and scared in a dark hole. He didn't know where he was.'"*

"That's good," said Michelle.

Sally went on.

"*'He was hungry but he was unhurt.'"*

"Right."

"*'The beast was nowhere to be seen'"*

"Good."

"*'Toby wondered where it had gone and why it had left him there alone. He stood up and walked around. When his eyes had accustomed to the darkness, he saw in the shadows that the beast had not left him but was there still, sleeping in the corner.'* Erm..."

"How about '*the beast is dead*'?"

"What from?"

"Anything. It just dies."

"Alright. '*Toby waited but the beast didn't move. He accidentally kicked a rock and cried out but it still didn't move. He went closer to have a look and saw that the beast was not asleep, it was dead.'"*

"Then he could escape and get back to civilisation again."

Sally ended the story with everyone except the beast in perfect health.

"Now what?" Michelle asked.

"Now we have to get Mr Jarvis to read it aloud. He read the first story so he has to read this one, too. If someone else reads it, it might be a different beast and all kinds of things go wrong. It has to be him."

But the next day, when they presented their teacher with the story and asked him to read it aloud, he wouldn't. In fact he looked a bit peeved.

"We talked about this already, Sally," he said. "I thought you'd changed your mind about this whole silly notion."

"I did a bit, sir, but you never know."

"I do know!" said Mr Jarvis. "What's happened to Toby is a serious thing, Sally. I can't make light of it by reading out a story to get him back again. It won't work."

"There's no harm, sir."

"Yes there is. It would be wrong of me to try because I don't believe it. If you really want to help, you'd do what the police asked and see if you can remember anything that might be of use to them."

They pleaded with him and could see he was upset that he wouldn't do what they asked, but he was adamant.

They did their best to work normally, but couldn't concentrate. Toby's disappearance was a horrible shock and they all felt vulnerable, beast or no beast.

Friends

Sally sat on the floor, arms clasped around her knees, watching television in a bit of a dream. She was bumped out of the dream when the program presenter handed over to the newscaster for the latest 'national and international' news.

"*Police are still searching for eleven year old Toby Tinker who disappeared from his home last week.*"

Sally sat up straight and concentrated on the television screen.

"*Chief Superintendent Maddox who is in charge of the investigation said that at the moment they have very few leads and are keeping all options open. Anyone with information should contact the police immediately. Toby was last seen wearing blue jeans, a green jumper and black anorak. This is a recent photograph.*"

The photo made Sally jump. There on screen was the face of the boy in her class who was so much a thorn in the side of everyone who knew him yet who they all wanted safe and back amongst them as soon as possible.

The news broadcast ended with another call for

anyone who recognised Toby and who might have seen him since his disappearance to telephone the police on the number shown. Some kind of talent show came next and Toby vanished from view.

"It's a terrible thing to happen," said Sally's mother, who had watched the broadcast from the doorway.

"Do you think he's alright?" Sally asked.

"I hope so, love. You have to keep hoping."

"There was something about him, mum," said Sally. "He wasn't bad or nasty like some of the others, but he was always in trouble. He couldn't read or write and he never stopped talking. There was something wrong and no one could put it right."

Sally's mother gave her a cuddle and said, "There must have been a reason he was like that. Lots of children are naughty, but they're not bad, and they don't deserve this kind of thing happening to them. Poor boy."

Sally desperately wanted to tell her mother about her story of the beast and of all the other things she'd written which had come true. She wanted to know if this bad thing happening was her fault. She'd never spoken about them before but knew for certain that her mother would say exactly the same thing as Mr Jarvis. There was, she decided, no point. The television announcement had upset her, but it had also given her an idea.

There was something else she could do.

Go back.

Down there.

She had to!

But would she have to go alone? They'd all been warned off and her friends wouldn't just say yes because they liked each other. In fact, Jackie almost certainly would say no. All their parents had given them fair warning about doing foolish things in a dangerous world, but Jackie's had been particularly clear and there was no way she'd do the same thing again.

Michelle might, though. She seemed less fazed by adults than Jackie. So when they next met, Sally was surprised when Michelle said, "Not on your life, Sal! Are you nuts?"

"Once more, that's all."

"No way. No, no, no, no way."

"We won't get caught," said Sally. "I've thought about it. We can do it on Sunday. Nobody's around. And we can ask The Others."

The Others were Josh, Adam and Jo, brothers and sister. They didn't go to the same school but they'd been friends for ages.

Michelle was upset. She didn't want to say no to her best friend, but she didn't want to get into trouble.

"They won't come."

"Why not?"

"Because they're not stupid, Sal. Why should they?"

Sally was quiet for a moment then told Michelle what was on her mind.

"There's something down there," she said. "I

know it. If it's the beast, it listens to the things in my head. Right deep down things that you never talk about and I have to find it. If I get annoyed with someone, or they upset me, then it starts, and we all get annoyed with people some time. Don't you ever wish horrible things that you don't mean?"

"Suppose so," said Michelle, not sure whether to worry more about the beast, her friend or herself.

"So do I. Look, I know this is wrong, and I know there's a chance we'll get into trouble, but I have to go back. There's really something there!"

"Something? What something, Sally? There's nothing. If we do it and we get caught we could get expelled."

They didn't argue, but Michelle wouldn't agree. She was almost in tears. She couldn't believe her best friend wanted to do the same stupid thing again, or that she'd asked her to join in. Nevertheless, they met up with Josh, Adam and Jo and told them everything that had happened.

"Everyone thinks I'm wrong," Sally said, "but I wrote the story and Mr Jarvis read it out in class and Toby disappeared."

"Sally thinks," said Michelle, "that stuff in her head, even secret stuff, comes true, like the beast, and she wants to stop it."

Josh thought about this for a full one second before saying, "Sally, you are bananas."

"No!" said Joanna crossly. Her brother could be annoyingly flippant just as she could be annoyingly earnest. "She's serious, can't you see? I've heard about people with powers like that. They can make things happen just by thinking about them. It's a true thing."

Josh and Adam thought Sally was a bit loopy but Jo didn't. She really took the whole thing seriously, and that made them wonder.

"So what do we do if we find this beast?" asked Adam.

"I think it will listen to me," said Sally.

"You think! What if you think wrong?" Adam was a bit edgy now.

"I'm going to do something to make it vanish. Forever."

What that was she never said, but Joanna was all for it. She was twelve years old and desperate for something exciting to happen. She read a book a day and her head was full of ideas. This was the real McCoy.

"Words of power," she said, "that's what it is. Words of power can do magic things. But they have to be spoken by witches or wizards."

"She's not a witch," said Josh, and then added, rather hesitantly, "is she?"

Even he was starting to get funny thoughts in his head about the girl with such a curious tale to tell and who told it with such conviction.

"Not like in books," said Joanna, "but there are witches around today. White witches who do good things. They meet in convents, or something like that, I don't know exactly, but they get together on Saturday nights and make magic. Sally might be a white witch."

A white witch! Was this what she was? Sally's heart skipped a beat. She was so glad she'd asked The Others to come. They would do it, she knew they would!

"Sounds crazy to me," said Josh.

"No," said Jo. "It isn't."

Josh looked puzzled, trying to work things out for himself but getting confused. He'd always believed that his sister knew best. This didn't feel like 'best' to him, though.

"I'll go," said Joanna. "Sounds great."

"I dunno," said Adam. "I'm thirteen. I'm too old to go looking for monsters."

"Me too," said Josh.

"You're scared," said Joanna.

"No we're not," the boys said together.

"Well, come then! What's the worst that can happen?"

The worst that could happen, they each thought, was worse than they could imagine, so they didn't try imagining it.

Silence for a few moments, then Adam asked the very question he shouldn't have asked because it sealed the decision. He said, "What if we get caught?" and immediately knew he'd made a big mistake. Joanna looked at him as though he was the biggest chicken on Earth and there would be only one way to prove her wrong.

"Okay," said Adam, "but it's nuts."

"Josh?" asked Joanna.

"Suppose so."

"Michelle?"

Michelle couldn't make up her mind whether or not Sally had some mysterious gift, but seeing the way the group was heading, she didn't want to be left out.

"Alright," she murmured, and as the words came out of her mouth, she had pictures in her mind of her mum and dad and every teacher screaming blue murder. She tried to put the thoughts aside.

"That's it then, Sally," said Joanna. "We're in."

So, despite all the advice from every sensible grown-up she knew, clever Sally Shakespeare had come to the wrong decision and convinced her friends to join in and suffer the consequences. She wasn't happy about it, but she had to find out the truth.

Whatever was bothering her, for best or beast, she needed to do this.

Gloom

Sally's school was situated in a quiet, woody area of London. Two sides looked out onto terraced houses, but being a Sunday there were very few people around. The third side was edged by a narrow road with a large, grassy area opposite, while a wood bordered the fourth. On this last side trees came right up to the perimeter fence and hid it almost completely from public view. The children gathered at the edge of these trees and looked through the fence into the playground.

"Still time to change our minds," said Josh.

"What, now?" exclaimed Joanna, "after bringing all this stuff and getting all worked up? Never!"

'All this stuff' was not a great deal - some torches, candles and matches ('You never know' Michelle had said) and more bait. They also had some extra clothing as the boilers would probably be switched off over the weekend and the rooms were bound to be cold. Finally there were some gloves and knee pads for crawling and two trowels for moving loose stonework. Considering they had little idea what they were going to find, they had used as much forethought as possible.

"I feel like a thief," said Michelle.

"But you're not," replied Joanna. "We're not going to take anything, are we?"

"But it's breaking and entering," said Adam, "and that's illegal."

"We've been through that already," said Joanna. "We won't get caught, but even if we do, we're doing this for all the right reasons. True?"

She asked in such a forceful way that made contradiction impossible. "Let's start then," she said. "Go on, Josh. We'll keep watch."

Josh's father worked in a garage and Josh had borrowed a strong pair of wire cutters. He put on a pair of gloves, took out the cutters… and hesitated.

"Well, go on!" Joanna was impatient.

"Alright, alright."

Josh looked left and right, then across the playground to the terraced houses and could see no one. He crept up to the fence and began to snip. The mysterious hole that had appeared the day Toby disappeared had been repaired and reinforced, but the rest of the fence wasn't too hard to cut.

"That's not high enough," Joanna said.

"You do it then," said Josh, "it's high enough for me and it's high enough for you. We don't want a great big hole that any Tom, Dick or Harry can see."

He was cutting a semi-circle from the base of the

fence, about thirty centimetres high at its peak.

"We'll cut our necks on it," insisted Joanna.

Josh muttered something rude under his breath but Joanna didn't hear. The others watched him attentively.

Suddenly, "Back!" called Michelle. "Back!"

Across the narrow road, along the edge of the field, a couple appeared, hand in hand. They stayed on the other side of the road and were walking away from the children who watched them pass in silence.

"Okay," said Joanna, "they're gone."

Josh went back to the snipping until the hole was finished, or at least he thought it was.

"Not yet," said Joanna. "There's still a bit more to go."

"I don't want to take the piece out completely," said Josh. "This is a hinge. Look. You can pull it back and fix it into place again. No one will know we've been in. Okay?"

"Smart," whispered Adam.

Michelle said, "Over there, that's the entrance to the boiler room staircase. We can run straight to it from here. You're only in view of the caretaker's house for a couple of seconds. If we run fast, he'll never see us. He's probably out anyway."

Actually, the caretaker was in, but being Sunday afternoon he was sleeping peacefully in front of the television.

"You go first, Jo," said Josh. "You're mad keen about doing this."

Joanna looked at her brother defiantly then

slipped away. She crept up to the newly cut hole, crawled through, checked the coast was clear then raced across the playground and disappeared down the stairs.

"Sal, you next," said Adam.

Now that it came to her turn, Sally was terribly aware of all the people she was letting down by this bad behaviour, but she was in too deep to back down so she followed Joanna. Michelle went next, then Adam, muttering to himself, "This is nuts." Josh went last, closing the wire gate as best he could afterwards.

The caretaker had thankfully not yet replaced the lock on the boiler room door. They got in the same way as the last time.

"Not exactly Fort Knox, is it?" said Adam.

"Sssh!" ordered Joanna. "Which way, Sal?"

Sally led them into the first room. There was something odd about revisiting it. It took on less of a menacing aspect than before, but for Michelle the close, musty airlessness brought back all the fears she thought she'd left behind.

"Light!" she whispered.

Sally and Adam switched on their torches which they'd wrapped in muslin to muffle the beams that barely lit up a metre of space. The dark remained largely untouched.

"You lead," said Joanna to Sally.

Sally led them through the first room, through the second and into the third. Very little light filtered down from the chinks in the ceiling and they virtually clung to one another in the isolating shadows.

"It's just like you said, Sal!" Joanna exclaimed in an excited whisper.

They listened, half expecting the sudden roar of a mad, bad beast whose secret lair had been invaded, but they heard nothing, just the soft hiss of water in the system and the usual odd building creaks and groans as atoms of bricks and mortar shifted ever so slightly.

"So what do we do now?" asked Josh.

"Use the bait," said Sally.

Michelle put out the cat food as they'd done before and the five of them sat in a corner of the room, waiting.

"Nothing here, Sal," said Joanna after a few minutes. "Why don't we spread out and look around?"

"I am not going anywhere down here by myself!" said Michelle.

"Why not?"

"Because I'm scared silly," said Michelle with great honesty.

The third room was much bigger than the other two. Many bits and pieces had been dumped in it and the children had to be careful not to bang their shins on old planks of wood and lengths of piping lying around.

"There's nothing down here," called Josh, "except rubbish."

It seemed that way to the others too, but then

Adam saw the deeper shadow to one corner and pointed. They shone a torch beam towards it and realized it was an open access to another room. They tiptoed through, shining the light here and there and saw piles of boxes and crates, covered in dust.

"It's some kind of storeroom," said Adam.

In one corner, they saw yet another deeper shadow and realised they were in a network of rooms, all wrapped in shadows.

"They go on forever," said Josh.

"Not forever," said Joanna, "but we better remember where we are or... well, let's just remember."

She fought fears of being trapped there forever.

They tried to remember, but it was easy to get disoriented in the maze of rooms. Some were big, some were quite small, some had boxes and bric-a-brac in them and some were empty. The school wasn't that old, but it had been built over older foundations, so this area might have been used once for other purposes. Two of the rooms allowed access to boilers, the others had been forgotten.

"I don't want to go any further in," said Michelle.

Joanna disagreed. If there was a beast down here, it would hide in the furthest rooms. It wouldn't skulk about near the main entrance. The others were undecided. They were all nervous, but they'd come so deep, they didn't want to pull out yet, but they had fears of being trapped down there till the end of time, and that was not a pleasant thought.

They managed to explore five rooms before disaster struck.

Adam had been tracing the boiler pipework that ran along the ceiling then up every now and again into the school main building. Set into the ceiling in the far corner of the fifth room was an access hatch. He pointed to it and Joanna's eyes lit up.

"No!" said Michelle. "Don't do it!" she said, reading her friend's mind.

"Just a peak," said Joanna. "There's nothing down here, so maybe it's up there. Come on brothers, give me a lift up."

Josh and Adam joined hands and Joanna stood on them while Sally and Michelle shone torches on to the hatch.

"Bit higher," called Joanna.

"You're too heavy," said Josh. "Can't you go on a diet?"

"Just a bit higher," insisted Joanna.

The two boys heaved as hard as they could as Joanna stretched up to try and push the hatch open.

"Careful," said Josh.

"I'm alright," Joanna called back in a strained voice.

"What can you see?" asked Michelle.

"My nose is on the edge. Push me up a little higher."

The boys did the best they could and Joanna managed to press the hatch open a couple of inches.

"Pitch dark," she said. "Hand me a torch."

Michelle gave the torch to Adam who tried to

give it to Joanna, but as she attempted to take it, the three of them tottered and Joanna felt the wall she was pressing against start to give way.

"Oh, oh!" she cried, which was the last sound the others heard before they were rained on by a mass of falling plaster. Joanna tumbled to the ground with a yelp and the others just buried their heads in their hands to protect themselves from the dust and debris.

The dust flew around like some kind of weird snow storm, tickling their eyes and throats. They coughed and spluttered and tried to wave away the millions of particles that hung around them.

"What have we done?" wheezed Adam through the thick white fog.

"Plaster's gone," said Josh. "You alright Jo?"

Jo lay on the floor looking like an angry ghost, covered completely in white powder.

"I feel like a… ow!"

As she started to stand, her left foot gave way beneath her with a sharp, unbearable pain and she cried out as she fell.

"Jo, what's wrong?" asked Michelle.

"My ankle. Oh!"

They stared for a moment in horror as Joanna fought back tears.

"I think I've broken it!" she wailed angrily, furious at herself for being so clumsy.

"This would happen, wouldn't it," said Josh.

"I didn't do it on purpose, Josh!" Joanna scolded him.

"Sorry Jo," said Josh, kneeling down next to her but not knowing what to do.

"What now?" asked Michelle, both distraught and furious, mainly at herself. "Can't you walk at all?"

Joanna tried to stand again but the ankle collapsed and the pain increased.

"I don't believe this!" said Adam.

"Well you better," said Joanna, "because it's true."

"Shall we get a doctor?" asked Michelle.

"Don't be daft," Josh said. "Let everyone know what we've been doing? They'll turn us into mincemeat."

"We'll get out of it somehow," said Sally feeling responsible for the whole terrible mess. "Look," she said, "there are some rags lying around. We can tear them up and use them as bandages. We need to wet them first. Cold is supposed to make the pain go away."

"Oh!" cried Joanna. "Take my shoe off someone! It really hurts."

Sally took Joanna's shoe off carefully and then her sock.

"Oh, hell!" exclaimed Adam as he saw Joanna's ankle. It was red and blue and swollen to twice its normal size.

"It's getting worser," said Joanna, throwing grammar to the wind. "Can't you do something?"

"We're trying, Jo," Michelle said.

"There's a tap outside," said Sally. "I saw it as

we came in. Just by the door. You can wet the rags there. Come on Michelle."

The two girls went through the other rooms back to the main door.

They didn't speak as they hurried through the network of rooms, but Sally knew that Michelle was angry. She also felt that some perverse force made things go wrong when you most needed them to go right.

They wet the rags and took them back to Joanna. The boys had propped her up against a wall, but she was in agony.

"Here," said Sally. "I'll wrap these around. They're very cold. Ready?"

"Ready.... oooh!"

Sally did what she could to tie the make-shift bandages around Joanna's foot as neatly as possible.

"How's it feel? Is it less painful?"

"A bit. Do it again."

Sally and Michelle honed their nursing skills, soaking the rags and wrapping them around Joanna's ankle. The others sat quietly and edgily, wishing they were a hundred miles away. Joanna took deep breaths and tried to calm down.

"I could do with a nice cup of tea," she said.

Sally did her best to do the right thing now, but she blamed herself for the accident and wondered how she could have been so stupid as to get them all into such trouble. 'This wasn't part of the story,' she said to herself. Nor was it. In fact, the whole story of the beast seemed to have lost credibility in the panic of the moment, and it would have been ridiculous to bring the subject up had not something happened which brought it back, horribly real.

From somewhere not too far off, there came a scratching and scrabbling sound.

"What's that?" asked Adam.

"Oh, no!" whispered Michelle.

"Sssh! Listen!" Josh ordered.

They were silent, scared to death and totally focused.

The noise came again, unmistakable. Something was moving, not far from them.

"Is it a rat?" asked Sally.

"Too big for a rat."

"What is it, then?"

"Ssh!"

They listened.

There it was again.

"It's the beast!" said Joanna. "We've got to get out of here. Now!"

"Can you move?" asked Josh.

"Oh! I'll try."

Joanna bravely pushed herself up, but the pain was terrible.

"Make a chair," she said.

"A what?"

"A chair. With your hands. You know. Two of you grip each other's wrists. That's it."

Adam and Josh held on to each other's wrists and knelt down as Sally slid the chair under Joanna who put her arms around her brothers' shoulders.

"Oow!"

"Sssh!"

"I can't help it."

"Is it any closer?"

They listened.

For a moment it seemed the noise had stopped but then it began again. A crawling noise.

"Come on, let's go," said Josh. "You alright, Jo?"

"No I'm not. I'm scared silly. Go!"

Michelle and Sally held the torch, Sally in front, Michelle behind the two boys and Joanna. They threaded their way through the rooms to the main door and breathed a sigh of relief to reach the fresh air and relative safety. The two boys gingerly sat Joanna down on the bottom stone step and caught their breath.

"We're not out of this yet," said Josh. "We've got to get across the playground and through the gap. Can you do it, Jo?"

"No, I can't. You'll have to carry me again."

"Can't you hop?"

"No I can't hop! My ankle's broken. You've got to carry me."

"Alright, alright. Ready?"

They remade the chair and lifted Joanna, but as they were about to run across the playground, Joanna said, "Oh no! I've left my shoe in there!"

"What?"

"My shoe. It's in there. If they find it, they'll know we've been here. You have to go and get it."

The others looked at each other.

"I'll go," said Sally. "I'll be alright. I'll meet you in the trees. Go on."

The two boys climbed the stairs slowly and when they reached the top they looked around, checking that the coast was clear.

"Okay?"

"Okay."

And they ran as quickly as they could, carrying Joanna who bounced up and down trying not to scream. When they reached the hole in the fence, they lowered Joanna and let her crawl through, following like soldiers on some secret mission.

Michelle waited at the bottom of the stairs for Sally to come back. 'Go and help her' a voice kept saying in her head, but her feet seemed rooted to the spot.

Inside, Sally tiptoed back to where the plaster had fallen, listening all the time. It was quiet again. Michelle's shoe lay covered in white dust. Sally stooped to pick it up. As she did so, something else caught her eye a little way off. At first, she wasn't sure what it was, but as she studied it, the crawling sound returned and she hurriedly put it in her pocket and stood up, ready to go. The beam from the torch shone against the dislodged hatch and lit up something that made her heart miss a beat.

Staring straight at her, reflected in the dust-filled amber light, were two sharp, glittering eyes.

Sally gave an almighty scream. The eyes disappeared and she ran from the room, tripping over everything and bruising her legs but reaching the door in one piece where she bumped into Michelle.

"What..?"

"Go!"

"What?"

"Just go! Now!"

Michelle looked into the dark room but saw nothing. She looked back at Sally then turned and fled across the playground. Sally banged the boiler room door shut and chased after Michelle, catching her up and almost beating her through the hole in the wire.

"What was all that about?" asked Michelle when they had caught their breath.

"Sorry," said Sally. "I..."

She didn't know what to say. She wanted to cry but she wouldn't, not in front of the others. Whatever it was Sally had seen, or had seen her, it was Joanna who needed their immediate attention.

"Look," said Adam, "Jo's in a bad way and we've got to get her home. We'll carry her to the park, then I'll phone dad. I'll tell him something or other. You two clean yourselves up and go home. Nobody must know what's happened. Okay?"

"Okay," said Michelle.

Sally nodded, but all she could think about were two pinpricks of light.

"Go on," said Joanna. "Do as Adam says. It's a good idea. I'll be alright."

"You sure?"

"Don't worry. Go!"

Sally apologised for the hundredth time, then she and Michelle dusted each other off and headed home.

Hope

Sally lay on her bed staring up at the ceiling, holding the thing she'd picked up from the boiler room the day before. She turned it around in the palm of her hand, concentrating so hard that, as if by thought alone, it would eventually tell its secret. She kept checking it to make sure she wasn't wrong, but no, there it was, a tiny silver locket on a chain.

If it was really his, really and truly... Sally's head spun, imagining what it meant.

A ring at the door bell, her mother's voice then footsteps; a few seconds later the bedroom door opened and Jackie came in.

"Hello," Sally said as cheerfully as possible, though she would much rather not have had visitors at that moment. Jackie looked miffed and asked, "Why didn't you ask me to go with you?"

"Where?"

"You know where!"

Sally didn't answer. It was one of life's awkward moments.

"Well?" asked Jackie again.

"You told us what your mum and dad said, Jackie. We didn't want to get you into more trouble."

"You could have asked." She went quiet then said, "I thought you were my friend."

"I am! It was a silly thing to do, you know that. You're lucky you didn't come."

Jackie was secretly glad, too, but still, not to be asked was worse.

"I suppose Michelle told you?" Sally asked.

Jackie's silence answered the question. She still looked peeved and now Sally was irritated with Michelle for telling, though it was a difficult secret to keep.

"I would have been able to help, if I was there," said Jackie.

Sally thought that if Jackie had come, it would have made matters worse. It was bad enough as it was, but who knows what would have happened if someone else had got hurt?

"You're not going again, are you?" Jackie asked.

Thoughts tumbled through Sally's mind. She felt bad already, but now she would have to lie for real.

"No. No reason to."

"Michelle said you saw something."

"Thought I did, but I didn't."

"So you won't go?"

"No."

Sally seemed to have decided that for the moment, it would be best to hold her tongue and say nothing. Secrets had a habit of not staying secret for long, and this had to be hers and hers alone, at least for a while.

They sat twiddling their thumbs, still peeved with each other for different reasons, Sally desperate to tell what was on her mind, but knowing that she wouldn't.

"No news about Toby," said Jackie, at last breaking the silence.

"No," Sally answered, biting her lip. She must have turned beetroot red.

"His picture was on TV again today," said Jackie. "He's on every day now. Do you reckon he's alright?"

Sally said she didn't know. How could she? All she wanted to do was find out for herself what was going on. It was so awkward with Jackie asking these questions.

"You seem... funny," said Jackie. "Different."

Sally knew she was being funny peculiar but she couldn't help it. She wasn't telling the truth and that made her uncomfortable.

"You going to tell your mum?"

"Tell her what?" Sally asked, panicking for a moment, thinking that Jackie knew more than she did. "Oh, right, you mean what we did? No, course not."

Sally felt horrid. Lying to her mother and father and friends was the worst feeling. A lie was like a seed; it grew and grew, only not into anything worth looking at.

"She'll be angry if she finds out."

"Well she won't find out. I don't want to talk about it. Can't we talk about something else?"

Jackie went quiet. She couldn't think of anything else to talk about.

"Thought you'd want to, that's all."

"Well I don't."

"Alright, alright."

Sally sat up, all agitated. Jackie perched herself on a chair and looked morose, knowing she'd been left out of something important and still not being properly let back in again.

"On the news they said they were looking for a blue sports car with a black cloth roof," she said.

"Every day they've got something new to look for, but they don't know anything," said Sally.

"How do you know? They might."

"If they knew, they'd have found him by now."

What she didn't want to tell Jackie, or anyone, was that she thought she knew something that no one else knew, and that all the other nonsense was just that, nonsense. Now why exactly she didn't head straight off to her parents and the police to tell them, she couldn't say. Sally Shakespeare had her own ideas about everything and wanted to do things her way. She'd always been taught to trust herself, and that's what she was doing now, trusting a tiny instinct which was telling her not to say a dickybird. Besides, she absolutely daren't tell anyone that they'd sneaked down to the boiler room yet again, not after the first awful warning.

Instead, she asked, "How long can people live without anything to eat or drink, Jackie?"

"I don't know! That's a weird question, Sally."

"Just wondered. If Toby was alive somewhere, I wonder how long he could live if he didn't have any sustenance."

"I don't even know what that means."

"It means food and water. How long can people survive without it?"

Jackie shrugged. She had much more desperate thoughts about Toby than Sally and she didn't think that 'sustywhatsit' was going to be his problem. For Jackie, he could have been anywhere on Earth and could beg, borrow or steal to eat, but for Sally he was in just one place on Earth and had nothing to beg, borrow or steal. She wasn't sure, of course, but the feeling was strong.

Jackie wanted to talk about him more than Sally, so Sally let her talk. She said that although they'd all said terrible things about him, she knew he wasn't a bad boy.

"I liked him, in a way," she said. "He was a teddy bear. A nutcase , but cuddly."

"Why do you keep saying 'was'? He could still be alive."

"Alright, he *is* a nutcase. I don't get him at all, but he mustn't be dead. That would be too horrible."

It was growing dark outside the window. The feeling between them was improving slightly, and despite Jackie being peeved still, there were more important things, and a missing Toby Tinker was one of them.

It often made more sense to tell people things rather than keep them locked up in your head all the time. Sally found it very hard to decide what to do, but a voice inside her kept saying 'Don't, don't! Not yet!' So she didn't, and by the time Jackie left, they'd half made up, but the other half would probably be done the next day or the day after that.

Sally hadn't said a word, but her worries seemed to show because her father said, "Anything wrong, Sal?"

"No. Everything's good, dad."

"You look... preoccupied."

"That's usual for our Sally, isn't it?" her mother asked, stroking her hair. "But especially now."

All the parents were suddenly even more protective of their children than before. When one child disappeared, they all felt vulnerable, and no matter how difficult things were at home, they all loved their children a little more than before Toby vanished.

"Everyone's upset," said Sally, feeling more and more guilty every second. She had no idea why she didn't tell her parents what was on her mind. This whole thing could be ended simply and quickly and they might even all be forgiven. But what if she was wrong? She'd just get into more trouble for nothing.

What was worse, she had to keep the lie going, to build on it like a house on rotten foundations, which was why she asked her mum and dad if she could leave home earlier in the mornings so that she could go to a reading club which Mr Jarvis was starting.

She needed time to go back down to the boiler room yet again, only now she would go alone. Last time, promise, to be sure once and for all what was happening. Then she'd tell people and everything would be back to normal.

Her parents were delighted that she was so keen, and they also thought a little more of Mr Jarvis. He had to be a good teacher if he got to school an hour early to run a book club!

Sally felt relieved and terribly guilty. She wanted to run and hide, but she was in too deep to turn back.

"You'll have to be up at half seven."

"That's alright."

"Every day?"

"Well, perhaps only twice a week. Mr Jarvis isn't sure yet."

Sally went to bed early. She tried to read a little but couldn't turn her mind to the story she was reading; real life was far stranger than any story she'd ever read, and so much more uncertain. You could never turn to the last page to see what would happen and worse, you couldn't be sure of a happy ending.

"You going to sleep now, Sal?"

Her mother had come up to kiss her goodnight.

"Yes."

"You look so troubled. Are you sure everything is alright?"

Poor Sally was so close to spilling everything that was on her mind, but something inside stopped her. "I'm alright," she said.

"Worried about Toby?"

"Everyone is."

"Let's hope he's alright," said her mother. "There's always hope."

"That's true, isn't it mum?"

"Yes, sweetheart, most of the time it is."

"So he might be safe and well?"

"Of course."

"Just because I wished him dead, he might not be?"

"No, of course not! You shouldn't think that, ever. We all say and do silly things when we're growing up, even when we're grown up! People can be silly and selfish, Sally, but you're not. You're a good girl and we're proud of you."

If any words were sure to make her feel worse than ever, these were those words! Poor Sally was so upset, but she managed to whisper, "Goodnight, mum."

"Goodnight, lovely Sally. Sleep well."

Invisible

Sally arrived at school around 7.45, an unearthly hour even for the keenest pupils. There were no other children around and she went unobserved straight to the entrance of the boiler room and down the stairs. She slid open the lock, pushed the door ajar and slipped inside.

Whether or not it was the results of her preparation, Sally was for some reason less scared than she'd feared. Though she'd been here twice before, it was never alone. Nevertheless, something inside kept her calm and prepared. The worst thing was not fear itself, but the fact that, despite all her deliberations, she knew she was doing the wrong thing, that it was against the wishes of almost everyone who cared about her. She just hoped that somehow everything would turn out alright in the end, that what she was doing was more important than all the trust that had been placed in her.

She switched on her torch, covered as before with soft muslin. The light it shed was also soft, casting gentle shadows on the walls, the floor and the great, copper boilers, humming away as the scalding heat flowed into a network of pipes, warming the schoolrooms with their high ceilings and cold, brick walls. The drums were huge, towering above little Sally Shakespeare, looking down on her like angry giants, wondering who this was invading their home.

Once the door was shut, it was difficult to believe that it was barely eight in the morning, that it was light outside and that school would soon begin. However would she concentrate on lessons after this? Assuming she got out alive.

She moved inside and stopped, listening more carefully to each sound than she had ever listened to anything or anyone in her life, and watching with the eye of a hawk. In her mind she heard her mother pleading with her not to go further, the disbelief of her father who imagined his Sally could do no wrong and the disappointment of all her teachers.

So why was she there?

She was there because a story had been written better than hers. It had a plot that left no other option but for Sally Shakespeare to solve the mystery alone. Adults wouldn't listen. Friends were scared and couldn't be asked to do more than they had done. The idea of the story was far stranger than her own and she had to find out whether or not it was true.

She moved into the second room. It was very warm now. The boilers must have been turned on at an early hour; perhaps left on all night. Some hissing sounds came through the dark as drops of boiling hot water fell to the ground, turning into steam. Her feet came close to the sizzling pipes and she felt the heat cross the air to make her skin tingle. There was a distinct smell in the air of damp, dust and fading memories.

Sally shone the torch up to the ceiling, around the walls and along the floor. She saw footprints which were probably, but not certainly, those of the school keeper. She wondered if, when he came down to check the boilers, he'd seen the prints they all must have left, and if he'd suspected anything. But it had been a while now and nothing had been said. This time she would cover up her steps. If he came down and saw her, what would she do? Shining the torch around she picked out places to hide, but it wasn't easy.

The room with the hatch - there it was, shut again, out of reach. Rubbish lying around, the planks of wood, the boards, old buckets, bits of piping and plastic mouldings. She stepped over them and shone the torch on to the fallen wall. The plaster hadn't been touched. No one had been down to clean up the mess, or perhaps someone had seen it but decided it wasn't worth the effort.

The dust settled and she could see the area clearly. A part of the wall revealed by the broken plaster was old brick, grey, dirty and crumbling. Sally shone her torch on it. Nothing. She swept the beam across. At the bottom right hand corner was a hole about seventy centimetres in diameter. Sally squatted down and shone the torch inside. Silence. She listened hard but the only sound was a distant hum of the giant boilers.

She dipped her head down and squeezed through the hole, shining the torch around as she did so, her heart beating fast and furious. This was just about the stupidest thing she could have done, she knew that, but she couldn't stop herself. She had to find out.

The space was about five feet high, just enough for her to stand and feel her hair brush against the ceiling, but it was quite long and wide with a rough gravelly floor. In the centre, the ceiling bulged down a little, perhaps from damp seeping through after many years. The space was too shallow to be used for much but pipes had nevertheless been routed along one of the walls. Sally could feel its heat but she could barely see it, and if she turned off the torch, which she did just to check, the darkness was thick as pitch. She wanted to get out and get home, but she couldn't give up, not now.

In the lower left corner of one wall was a hole, about a body width in diameter. Sally squatted down and shone the torch into it. It seemed to lead into the heart of the school building. She could see the beam carve out a path quite high up, hitting woodwork and rafters before it disappeared about thirty feet away. She saw that it would be possible to squeeze up into these spaces and find your way like a spider into secret parts of the building.

Which is just what she did.

Beyond, the spaces opened out, the air was cooler and a little light filtered down from cracks and crevices. Sally turned off the torch, waiting a moment for her eyes to accustom to the dark. To her left she thought she could make out the shadow of a staircase but it was hard to be sure of anything, and she stood still, not wanting to knock anything over or make any noises. The hum of the boilers had disappeared. Instead, she heard sounds from above, footsteps, and faint knockings.

'Cleaners,' she thought to herself.

About this time, the cleaners were finishing up their work for the morning, trying to get things in order before the children rushed in to wreck it all. They were there now, vacuuming the classroom floors and school staircases, picking up endless black bags of rubbish and making the building ready for the day ahead. Sally had heard cleaners complain to the teachers about the 'state' some of the classes were in, but it didn't seem to matter; the mess was there every day waiting for them.

She heard the thump of the vacuum hoses dragged around, and when she concentrated she could hear the faint sound of voices. She could even hear, when the vacuums were off and the brooms, dustpans and brushes still, the distant chatter of... yes, Mrs Brown and Mrs Wilson, two cleaners who had been at the school longer than anyone.

Sally smiled to herself with a mixture of delight and guilt, 'It is them!'

For a moment she felt slightly safer.

She strained her ears to listen to what they were saying but could only catch a few words.

"Crab... rude... un... idy... oom."

Sally couldn't make out anything out for certain, but it was exciting to think that she could hear them and that they had no idea little Sally Shakespeare was there, eavesdropping, a spy in the dark.

She climbed back inside the shallow room but her hand hit the wall and she dropped the torch. Her sight had grown more accustomed to the dark now so she could see faint shapes, and one of these was a heap like a newly filled grave, in the far corner. The sound of the torch rolling away frightened her, and another sound rooted her to the spot, a rustling, sliding and shaking.

Sally silently squatted down, fumbling for the torch, but she couldn't find it. The more she searched, the more she lost her sense of just exactly where it had fallen.

She took a step back.

The movement from up ahead came again, this time a distinct shuffling of feet.

Sally tried to say something but her voice was dry and inaudible, her lips barely moving.

She waited a few moments and then slowly put one foot behind the other, trying to squirm backwards, at least the way she thought backwards should be.

Her foot caught on something and she tumbled over and lay still.

In her head she saw flashing visions of the beast jumping on to her, fangs and claws open, teeth dripping saliva, mouth wide open in hunger and anger at being disturbed like this.

But there was nothing.

Just silence.

After a few moments she tried to rest on her heels which were sore, but not badly hurt. She had fallen away from the wall and when she opened her arms to touch it there was nothing there.

Again she tried to take small, squatting steps towards where she thought the wall should be, but the blackness was deep again and she'd completely lost her sense of direction.

She squinted hard, trying to breach the extraordinary darkness, breathing as slowly as possible. Every moment she expected to be sprung upon, to see two green eyes piercing the darkness, staring at her with a malicious look of triumphant wickedness and evil.

The darkness remained unbroken.

She got into a crawling position and started to creep forward ever so slowly, but now forward and backward had no meaning and she couldn't tell if she were getting nearer or farther from the entrance.

With the loss of sight, her senses of smell and hearing were suddenly stronger as she sniffed and listened like a hunted animal.

The thought came to her that she might be lost there forever, that she would never find the way back, that after days of suffering she would die of hunger. A few moments before she had dreaded the school keeper coming down into the boiler room; now she prayed he would come, and soon!

She couldn't see any part of herself, not even her

hands if she held them a few inches from her face. Not her feet, her clothes, nothing. She might as well be invisible. Perhaps that was what it was. The beast had made her invisible like itself. It could see her, but no one else could.

"No, no, no," Sally kept on saying to herself, "it's just dark, that's all, dark."

There was this feeling almost of floating. Only the hard, cold floor kept her in contact with the lost world of real things which could be seen and touched. She wondered if she were to jump up, whether the floor, too, would disappear, like the wall, and she would float on forever into space.

Something snapped her back to reality.

A clicking sound and a dull, feeble beam of pale yellow, almost orange light appeared.

She froze and stared in the direction of the light. It moved, snaking around slowly, looking for her, searching her out, but not finding her. It was too weak and the beam faded and died a good five feet in front of her.

The beam moved again, this time not from a central point but around, as if the thing that was causing it to glow was also moving, gently, carefully, but definitely moving, forwards, backwards, to the left, to the right...

Sally closed her eyes to think hard and to summon up courage. It was funny how doing this helped, even though the darkness and the loneliness were as great with her eyes wide open as with them shut. She took a deep breath, trying to remember why she had come down here all alone, against the advice of the wiser adult world. There was no choice now, just the difficulty of actually doing it, of finding out, of measuring truth against imagination.

How hard that was!

Suppose she had been wrong all along? The fear of this didn't trouble her as much as it might. It was just the fear of facing up to truth and casting aside illusion. You could only live in your mind so long, the world had to be faced eventually or it would confront you when you were least ready. Better to be ready and in command.

But the fear of being wrong now was far worse, of facing up to something unexpected and possibly terrifying, of being proved wrong in every way!

Fatally wrong!

But she had to know!

Sally counted to three and whispered in a hoarse, dry voice, "Toby?"

Too soft; no answer.

Louder.

"Toby?"

Quiet, but an expectant quiet.

Sally waited, holding her breath, her heart beating fast, her mind fully concentrated on the terrible dark silence around her.

Suddenly, from somewhere not too far away came a sound like balm to a wound, a sound that seemed all at once to dispense with childhood imaginations, replacing it with the solid, equally mysterious quality of a grown-up wisdom. With that sound, the beast disappeared from her fancy forever. It was no longer a threat, no longer going to jump on her or take away her friends, teachers or family. It vanished in a puff of smoke back to the imaginary world from which it had sprung. She could laugh at it because it wasn't real. She knew it wasn't real. She knew how silly and stupid and babyish she had been and she regretted everything she had done to upset everyone. She regretted getting her friends into trouble. She regretted being the cause of so much concern and all for nothing but a childish idea that she should have left behind long ago. Whatever possessed her? How could she be so stupid?

She let out a deep breath and, even in the pitch black, sightless world of the lair, relaxed, all in one fleeting, life-changing second, because she'd heard a familiar word, one that would never be the same again, the word, "Boo!"

Jump

"Toby, is that you? It's me, Sally."

Quiet, then a whisper in the darkness.

"What you doing here?"

"Came to find you."

"How d'you know I was here?"

"I didn't know for sure. I'm so glad you're alive, Toby!"

"Course I'm alive. What d'you think?"

"Everyone thinks, well, they don't know, do they? Anything could have happened."

"Well it didn't. I'm here, init?"

Sally almost laughed with relief. She felt justified. A moment ago she was a villain, betraying everyone who loved her. Now she was a heroine who'd found The Lost Boy safe and sound. People would be astonished at how bright and brave she was!

"Can I see your face, Toby?"

The faint torch light, apparently from half-dead batteries, cast a pale beam upwards, lighting the face from below, but the light was so pale that Sally couldn't see much at all.

"It's no good," she said. "You'll have to come

closer."

"You got anyone with you?"

"No."

"Sure?"

"Yes. I'm alone."

"Alright. Keep talking."

Sally heard steps approach and she saw the weak beam of light grow gradually stronger and Toby's face appear from the gloom like a sickly ghost.

"Hello, Toby. I'm so happy you're alright."

Sally had held her breath again as Toby approached. It was one thing hearing the disembodied voice, it was another actually seeing that oh so familiar face close to her own, all shady and spooky in the weird light.

"You should not a come," said Toby.

"I had to," said Sally. "You're a TV star now. Everyone's talking about you. You've been on all the news programmes and everything."

"Why?"

"What do you mean, why? It's obvious."

Silence. Sally realised that Toby had no idea how people would react to his disappearance; he thought no one would take any notice!

"You can't just go missing and expect people not to try and find you. What about your mum and dad?"

"What about them?"

"Don't you think they'd miss you and want you back?"

"No."

Sally was unprepared for this. Her parents loved

her so much they would move heaven and earth to get her back if she disappeared. It seemed unbelievable that other parents could be so very, very different.

"Why?"

"Cos they wouldn't. Mind your own business, anyway."

Toby shuffled forward and Sally heard a clinking sound as his foot kicked her torch. She knelt, picked it up and turned it on. The beam was clearer than Toby's and she lit him up in his full untidy glory.

"Ow, not in my eyes, stupid!"

The sight of him made Sally jump, inside if not outside.

"Toby! You look terrible! Have you been in here all the time? Alone in the dark?"

"Might have been."

"But... but why?"

"I'm not going to tell you, am I?"

"But you'll tell the others won't you?"

"What others?"

"The class. Your mum and dad. The police."

"I ain't tellin' no one. Don't be daft."

"But when you see them you'll have to tell them."

"I ain't gonna see them, am I?"

Sally had taken it for granted that Toby would come out with her, now that he'd been found. It hadn't occurred to her that he wouldn't want to come with her. That didn't make sense.

"I ain't gonna come out just cos you found me.

And you mustn't tell no one neither."

"But why? I thought you'd want to come back with me."

"Well I don't."

"Suppose I tell them?"

"I'll run away for real. You won't find me next time."

"I don't understand. It's horrible down here. You must want to come back. You can't stay in this place for ever."

"I can if I want."

"But you'll die of hunger. And it'll get cold."

"I'm alright. I get things."

"What things?"

"Things I need."

"How?"

"Ain't tellin. Just do."

Sally was puzzled, trying to work out what it was that could make Toby prefer this dark lonely hole to the world outside, but she couldn't.

"How d'you find me?" asked Toby.

Sally started to explain, then stopped, having forgotten for a moment where she was and the time of day. Up above, in the strange reality she'd left behind, school was about to start.

"Look," she said. "I have to go. You know what the time is?".

"About nine, init," said Toby.

"How do you know that?" asked Sally, surprised.

"I got a watch," said Toby, "over there. And other stuff. Not much, but enough."

He pointed to the heap of rags where he'd made a rough bed on the rougher floor. Sally had to admire the boy, even though he was just about last at everything and a trouble to everyone, he'd made a little home here and kept himself safe and sound. He even knew what time it was.

"I have to go," said Sally. "You know that. It's time for school."

"Don't you tell anyone about me," warned Toby.

"Why?" asked Sally.

"If you come back alone after school, I'll tell you. That's a promise," said Toby. "Bring a new battery for my torch. Bring somefing to eat. Then I'll tell you. You bring the police an' I'll know an' I'll get away."

Sally shook her head,

"I don't know if I can come back. It isn't easy, Toby."

"'bout five. Say you're going to a friend or somefing. Don't you bring no one, alright? No one. I'll hate you forever if you do."

Sally was aware of Toby's desperation.

"I won't," she reassured him, "but if I don't come, it's because I couldn't. Alright? Not because I didn't."

"Don't bring no one."

"Alright! You don't have to say it a million times! I get it."

"Which way out you gonna go?"

"Which way?" Sally was puzzled. "Is there another way?"

Quiet for a moment, then, "No. That way. Go on. I want 'C's."

"What?"

"Batteries."

"Oh, okay. I'll try."

"Two of them. And somefing to eat, somefing nice. A pair of socks, too. And a box of matches."

Sally looked at Toby and said, "How about a nice comfy chair and a TV set?"

"If you like. But you don't bring no one."

"No. No. No. No. No. I won't! You don't half go on, Toby, but I'm really glad you're alright, all the same. Honest."

Sally slipped out of the room, looking back at where Toby must have been standing, but seeing nothing.

"Bye," she called.

She waited for an answer.

"You really glad to see me?" came the gentle, hesitant reply.

"Course I am! Really and truly! You don't know how glad, Toby! Bye."

"Bye."

The voice was soft, sad and distant, not like the brash, crazy Toby she knew in class.

Sally hurried through to the main boiler room where she saw with relief and delight the chink of light from the doorway. Looking around cautiously, she crept out without anyone seeing and joined the growing mass of children in the playground.

Keyhole

"You alright, Sal?" Michelle asked.

"Fine. Why?"

"You look... I don't know... different."

"Do I? How?"

Michelle studied her friend as if she was looking at a picture in a book.

"You're pale. And your eyes are shiny."

"Bit tired, that's all."

Michelle took Sally's arm and said, "Did you see the news last night? They said Toby was seen in Newcastle."

"Newcastle? That's hundreds of miles away!"

"Well, they weren't sure. It might have been him."

Jackie was holding Michelle's arm. She said, "Didn't you see breakfast TV?" Sally definitely hadn't seen Breakfast TV. She'd been somewhere else entirely at the time. "It was on there."

"Bit of a way to go, Newcastle, isn't it?" said Michelle.

"He'd have been seen," said Jackie. "You can't travel hundreds of miles without being seen. What do you think, Sally?"

"How should I know?" said Sally, a little petulantly. She was bursting to say something. It was all she could do to hold her tongue and keep from giving away even the tiniest crumb of what she knew.

"Mum says she gets more pessimistic with every day that goes by," said Michelle, then explained to Jackie what pessimistic meant. "Hopeless and forlorn," she told her.

Sally tried not to smile. It would have been so out of place and heartless. She forced herself to remember that her friends were in that same state of anxiety and sadness that she herself had been in until a moment earlier. How hard it was to hide her feelings!

"You mustn't give up," Sally told them. "You have to keep hoping. Fact is stranger than fiction."

"You really are different," said Michelle. "Yesterday you thought he was, well, you know."

"Maybe I'm growing up," said Sally.

"You don't grow up in a day," said Michelle.

"Takes at least two days," said Jackie, and they laughed, for the first time since Toby had disappeared. Michelle and Jackie immediately felt guilty and stopped.

"It's wrong to laugh," said Jackie. "We shouldn't do it. Not till he's been found."

"What if he's, you know, never found?" Michelle asked. "Can we ever laugh again?"

"He'll be found," said Sally. The other two girls looked at her with puzzled expressions. "You have to keep hoping."

In their English class, Sally was determined to concentrate on her work, but when Mr Jarvis asked if she was feeling okay because she looked agitated, Sally flushed with worry. She was a little tired, she said, that was all. Her explosive secret was bubbling inside her like a volcano about to erupt. She did her best to focus but it was the hardest thing not to give away by a look or a careless word all that had happened. She was absolutely dying to tell them everything. 'I've found him! I've found him! He's alive! You won't believe it! He's in the boiler room! I found him!' "You dare!" she warned herself. "You dare!"

After lunch the police came. When Sally saw them, her heart sank. The police had a way of making her feel guilty even if she hadn't done anything. And she had done something! She started wondering if her meeting with Toby had been a dream. It seemed so unreal in the cold light of day. Was it possible that he was there now, that very minute, sleeping away peacefully in the dark recesses of the school? She shook her head in disbelief.

There were two police officers, a man and a woman, and they spoke to the whole school. The woman spoke very kindly, telling them what had happened and all the things they needed to remember to tell the police if they thought it was important. A few brave children asked questions, but it was all very solemn and serious. The children couldn't imagine anything more solemn and serious. No one was allowed to ask the police anything there and then, but they were told what to do if they had something important to say. Sally was on edge the whole time. She wondered why the police and indeed the whole school didn't point to her and say, 'Sally Shakespeare knows! Just look at her! She's guilty! Guilty! Guilty!'

When school ended, Sally was anxious to get back to Toby, but how should she do it? Her friends chatted with her and her mum was keen to make sure she was okay. Everyone was talking about the missing boy and every parent was worried about their own children. It would be hard to be alone for any length of time, and impossible, Sally decided, without a little white lie. Everything she'd been taught prompted her to tell her parents, the school or the police, but if she did, she'd be breaking her promise to Toby and he'd hate her forever or run away again, or both. After tea, then, she made a pretend call to Michelle so that her mother would hear, making fake arrangements to be there in five minutes.

"Be back by six o'clock for supper," her mother said.

"I will, mum."

She emptied her satchel and put into it her own torch, some matches, a cardigan and a couple of comics. Taking some money from her savings tin, she went to the corner shop and bought two rolls, some cheese slices, a Cornish pasty, a small cake, sweets and a can of fizzy drink. She also bought batteries for Toby's torch. By the time she was ready, her satchel was heavier than it was in school time.

At five o'clock, the school was still busy. A few teachers might still be around, a club or two could still be running and the cleaners would definitely be there. It would probably be impossible to dash in without looking suspicious and without being noticed. It would be safer instead, she thought, just to walk in and quietly make her way to the back of the school. If anyone was there, they wouldn't take any notice, and if she was questioned, she could always say she was looking for something she'd left behind. She wondered whether the more you lied, the easier or the harder it became.

Nearing school she breathed slowly and tried not to panic. She hurried around to the back of the building and down the stairs. Opening the door she slid in, closed the door behind her, switched on the torch and made her way forward.

It was strange, she thought, how now, the fourth time she'd been there, she felt no fear at all. She knew what lay ahead and threaded her way comfortably through the rooms. There was even an air of familiarity about the place, almost welcoming. Unknown things were nearly always scary, but knowledge took away the fear.

She crept up to the small access hole and shone the torchlight inside.

"Toby?"

Silence.

"Toby?"

Nothing.

She thought he'd be waiting impatiently for her, but no, all was silence and stillness.

She took off her satchel, slid it inside the access hole then squeezed in after and stood up, shining the torch light around. Toby wasn't there. For a moment Sally was angry, then disappointed. Had he run off for real, this time? Maybe he thought she'd bring the headmaster or the police with her. Where was he?

"Up here!"

The voice was a whisper, drifting down from the shadows above. Sally saw a chink of light in the low ceiling at the back of the room. It widened and she saw Toby's pale face staring at her.

"What are you doing?" she asked.

"Nuffing. Watching you."

Sally walked forward to see better. In the ceiling was a square hatch and Toby was lifting it up and peering down at her.

"It goes to the back of the stage," said Toby. "I'll come now."

He opened the hatch and lowered a dirty aluminium ladder to the ground, closed the hatch behind him and climbed down.

"I just wanted to make sure you were alone."

"I said I would be."

"I know. I just wanted to make sure. You ain't hiding anyone, are you?" asked Toby.

"No I am *not* hiding anyone," said Sally. "I came

by myself and I'm probably going to go to prison for doing this," she said.

Toby laughed. "No you're not," he said. "They don't send kids to prison!"

Just for a moment, Toby looked more like a little man than a little boy. Sally had the feeling that if anyone was hiding anything, it was him, hiding away much more in his peculiar head than people had given him credit for. She felt terribly sorry for him.

"I can't stay long," she said, "but I've bought a few things for you."

She took out the batteries and Toby put them in his torch. He flicked it on and admired the bright new beam.

"Here's some comics to read."

Toby thumbed through them silently.

"And a cardigan to keep you warm."

"It's a girl's one."

"Of course it is, it's mine."

Toby put it on.

"It's alright," he said.

"And some food."

No sooner had she taken out the food and drink than Toby started stuffing it into his mouth at a hundred miles an hour. He was starving. Sally watched him, fascinated, uncertain, full of pity. It was like peeking through a keyhole into a life she didn't understand at all.

He finished everything, despite Sally saying that he should keep a few things for later. He must have been famished. Sally gave him everything she'd bought, including the locket. Toby was amazed.

"Where d'you find that?"

"One of the rooms. It was half buried in the dust. That's how I knew you were here."

"I was looking for it everywhere. Thought I'd lost it for good."

"I don't think I've got anything else."

"Let's put it here with my other stuff."

Toby showed Sally where he kept the little that he had with him. All of it was tumbled together in a heap on the floor, underneath a messy pile of rags.

"How could you have stayed here a week without getting cold and hungry and fed up, Toby? It's so miserable. Why are you doing this?"

Toby stared at Sally for a moment, considered something, then rolled up his shirt and cardigan and turned his back to her.

Learning

Even in the dim light she could see the marks, healing, but still vivid.

"Who did it?" she asked.

"Who do you think?"

"I don't know."

"You are thick, sometimes."

"Tell me."

"Just cos your mum and dad like you don't mean all mums and dads like their kids."

"You mean...?"

Sally couldn't believe it. Her parents loved her so much she assumed all parents would feel the same. If not, why have children in the first place? It made no sense. Children could be naughty, but this? Why had they done it?

"They get fed up with me," said Toby. "Everyone does, and so do they."

To her dismay, Sally realised that this was true. Everyone in their class got fed up with Toby Tinker. He couldn't do anything right, he couldn't read or write properly and he was silly and noisy. But his mum and dad? They were different, surely!

"Haven't you told anyone?"

"Like who?"

"I don't know. Tell the teachers or the police. Yes, tell the police. They'll do something."

"Can't do that, can I? They're still my mum and dad."

"But they hit you!"

Toby wiped his eyes, but he was refusing to cry properly, not in front of anyone else.

"Dad lost some money at the betting shop and mum had been drinking. It weren't good. Then they both got angry at me for getting into trouble at school."

"Oh, Toby!"

Sally felt inordinately sorry for him. He was like a little teddy bear with the wrong owner. She realised once again how silly she'd been believing stupid things about her stories when in reality everything boiled down to the way people treated each other. It was so simple, and so complicated, too. She couldn't wait until she was grown up so she could sort it all out.

Toby started eating again. Sally watched him, wondering what it was best to do and to say. He couldn't stay there forever, but if she rushed him back, he'd run away, and she didn't blame him. She'd probably run away too if she got hit by people who were supposed to love her. It didn't make sense, but it happened. She looked around the dark, shallow room and said, "It's so miserable down here, Toby. You've got to get out. It isn't healthy."

"I do go out," he said. "I go out every night. I go

to the kitchen. I make myself a cup of tea and grab somefing to eat. Long as I don't muck anything, it's okay. There's always somefing there. Specially puddings. Loads of puddings."

"And no one sees you?"

"Who? It's late, and I don't use the light. Who's going to see me?"

"Aren't you scared?"

"Nah."

"I would be."

"Well, you're a girl."

"That doesn't matter," said Sally. "I came down here on my own, remember. I bet you're scared too, really." Toby had his mouth full and didn't answer. "Isn't it cold in here to sleep?" Sally asked him.

"A bit. But you get some heat from the boilers, so it ain't freezing."

"But why here, Toby? Why did you come here?"

"Seemed a good idea," he said. "I saw you girls come down here and get out alright, so I thought I'd come too. See if your beast was down here. I didn't fink it would be cos it didn't eat you, and anyway…"

"Anyway what?"

"It was only a story."

Sally was embarrassed. Was this all her fault?

"Yes," she said, "it was only a story. There's no beast, Toby. Not really. I made it all up."

"It was good, though," said Toby.

Sally could see that Toby was relieved. He might have been down in this horrid space for a while, but he was still nervous, just in case the beast was simply on holiday and about to return. She was amazed that he still thought about her stories despite all that happened to him. She wondered if other people were the same, believing in fiction because the real world could be so bad. She promised herself to write something happier next time.

Toby told her that there were ways out of the room into the school, besides the way she'd come. He'd found a different way back, and even a way out of the school itself.

"Isn't it locked?" Sally asked.

"I open a window when I go and lock it when I get back in."

"What do you do when you're outside, Toby?"

"Just things."

"What things?"

"My things. Don't be so nosey."

"Come on, Toby, tell me."

He wouldn't, so she guessed. It was a hard guess because it was something she would never do herself, but it came to her in a flash that the little boy in front of her probably wouldn't think twice about it.

"You steal, don't you?" she said. He said nothing in return. "That's wrong, Toby. You mustn't do that."

"I don't care."

"You'll get into trouble. Real trouble."

"Only if they catch me."

"They will catch you in the end."

"Only if you tell them."

"Even if I don't, they'll find you."

Toby opened the can of drink and started swilling it back.

"This is really good, Sally Shakespeare. You going to get me some more?"

Sally didn't answer for a moment. She found herself slipping into a world she didn't understand, of hurt children and runaways and stealing. And none of it was fiction, it was real as you like.

"I can't keep buying you stuff, Toby."

"Can't you pinch it?"

"No, I can't!"

"Why not?"

"You know why! Don't be daft."

"Just food and drink. I'll starve to death if you don't."

This was blackmail, but it might also be true. She ignored it for the moment and said, "What else have you got here?"

"Not much."

"Can I look?"

"If you like."

Sally poked around the heap of rags. Toby had made a bed from a large piece of sponge covered with a tarpaulin that he had found amongst the rubbish in the third room. The pillow was formed from a bag of sand which now bore the imprint of Toby's head.

"Can I tidy it up a bit?" asked Sally.

Toby shrugged as if he didn't care, but as he had

no sense of order himself, he was interested to see what Sally could do. She set about tidying the dismal sleeping arrangements, watched by Toby as if she was some kind of fairy godmother. When she'd done as much as she could, she said, "There. You'll be like a bug in a rug, now."

"What's that?"

"Cosy. You sure you don't want to come out with me? I bet the police could fix you a proper bed."

"Nah. I'm alright for a bit. Maybe in a while. Don't you go tellin' no one."

"I won't. What's this, Toby?"

Toby didn't answer, but he looked embarrassed. Sally had found an old bag and inside were...

"Books! Toby! Do you read them?"

Toby looked down. His cheeks were red but Sally couldn't see this in the gloom.

"It's hard," he whispered.

Sally imagined him poring over the books, guessing at words here and there, trying to understand what they meant. They were far too hard for him. He needed something simple, something easy to understand. She felt so sorry for him. She couldn't imagine her own life not being able to read.

"And what's all this?" In the same bag were exercise books and pencils. "Where did you get it all from?"

"One of the stockrooms. Where else?"

"Is it open?"

"Sometimes."

Sally began to see how Toby operated, taking what he could wherever he could to survive in his own secret world. She looked at the exercise books. They were full of squiggles and jumbled lines.

"There's nothing in them," she said, but as she said it, another flash of inspiration came. "You're trying to learn how to read and write, aren't you?" Toby shrugged. "You are, aren't you?" Sally said again.

"Maybe. It ain't that hard."

Sally could see that it was very hard and that Toby was trying to do by himself, in the dark, what should have been done at home and at school years before, in the light. She looked at him in a new way, full of respect.

"I've got some handwriting books," she said. "I can bring them tomorrow."

"I did a bit," said Toby, excited. "Look. S'a real mess."

He showed his scrawling efforts.

"No it's not. Some of it's good."

Sally was being kind and both of them knew it. Toby's attempts at writing were all over the place, as if a spider had dipped its eight legs in ink and gone for a crawl over the page. There were occasional patterns that looked like letters but mostly they were there by chance rather than design. Sally tried turning the paper around this way and that, but it didn't make much difference. The fact was that Toby couldn't write for toffees. Sally remembered some of the things she'd done way back in Years

Three and Four to learn how to write.

"You have to hold the pencil properly," she said, showing him, "and practise with patterns. You can start by doing things like this. Look."

She made some patterns on the page, zig-zags and curves.

"They're not real letters," objected Toby.

"It's just practise," Sally said. "Real letters come later. What you have to do is copy these exactly. Pages of them."

"How many pages?"

"Doesn't matter. As many as you like. You've got to make the pencil do what's in your head."

"There ain't nuffing in my head," said Toby, honestly.

Sally ignored this and said, "You need proper light. You'll hurt your eyes if you read and write in the dark."

"I've got this," said Toby, "but it ain't got no fuel." He took out a hurricane lamp from beneath the rags. "I borrowed it from a shop."

"You stole it, you mean."

"I needed it."

"Toby, what's wrong with you?"

"Nuffin."

"Look, if you want me to help, you've got to promise me not to steal anything more. Right?"

"Why?"

"Because it's wrong. That's why."

"What am I supposed to do? Go and ask for it?"

"Well, you shouldn't have run off like this in the

first place. It was a stupid thing to do. But now you're here I'll help a bit till you decide to come out, so long as you don't steal anything more. What you should do is put everything you've stolen on one side. Don't use it. Make a pile and forget about it."

"Even the lamp? We could use the lamp."

"Well, alright. We'll use the lamp, if I can get something to make it work. What else did you steal?"

"Bits and pieces."

"A lot?"

Toby showed Sally a knife, a woolly hat, a compass...

"A compass, what do you need that for?"

"Just in case."

"You don't need a compass down here. What else?"

He brought out about a dozen things he'd taken from a camping shop, very little of which he actually used.

"Put it all in a pile," said Sally. "When you come out again, it'll look better if they can see you're trying to be good."

"You're really bossy, you know that?"

"I'm not. I'm just sensible. Don't want to see you in more trouble."

"Why? Thought you didn't like me."

"I'm glad you're alive," she said, avoiding a direct answer. "But whether I like you or not, you're a lot nicer than Jonas Stamp."

"He hit me, you know."

"Yes, I know. And the police know, too."

"The police?" Toby asked, alarmed. "What do they want?"

"Toby," said Sally, a little bemused, "don't you have any idea of what's going on up there?" she pointed up to the real world that seemed so far away. Toby shrugged. "There are thousands of policemen looking for you," Sally told him, "all over the country. They don't know if you've been kidnapped, murdered or what. They're all wasting their time, aren't they?"

"Didn't ask them to look for me."

"But they're still looking. It's on the news every day. Pictures of you and everything."

"Don't care. Still ain't coming out."

"Tell you what," said Sally. "How about if you learn to write properly, if I teach you, then you come out. Is that fair?"

"What do you call properly?"

"Well, a story. One that a teacher can mark. No spelling mistakes, nice handwriting, interesting…"

"I'll probably be here for ever then," said Toby, disconsolately.

"Not if you practise."

"Yeh, yeh, yeh. Bossy boots. Alright."

"I have to go now."

"Why?"

"What do you mean, why? I have to."

"When you going to come again?"

Sally thought a moment.

"Tomorrow."

"Morning?"

"Maybe. It'll be difficult leaving home so early again. I'll try."

Toby went dreamy. He often did this in class when things were troubling him. His eyes became misty and he seemed to look inside himself. He was thinking that he would miss Sally when she left him, and he had never missed anyone before in his life, except his gran.

"I'll come," said Sally, reading Toby's mind.

"You better."

"You don't have to say that. I want to come."

"Honest?"

"Honest. You shine the torch on me as I go."

"Now?"

"Yes. I must."

Toby did as he was told.

"See you in the morning, then?"

"I'll try. If I don't come, it'll mean something has happened and I'll come in the evening instead, or when I can. It's not easy doing this, you know."

"Go on, then. See you tomorrow."

Sally left him and stepped out into the twilight of the late October evening. If she could have peeked back inside, she would have seen Toby, book and pencil in hand, feverishly copying lines of zig-zags and curves.

Maze

Sally had been surprisingly calm during the day. She thought she'd be bursting to tell everyone about Toby, but she wasn't. She was happy enough to keep the secret to herself and felt absolutely no wish to tell anyone, not Michelle, not Jackie, not the teachers nor the police; no one. This was her secret, and everything good depended on helping Toby in the way he wanted. She said nothing to her parents, just made plans in her head about the things she could do to teach the Lost Boy, as she thought of him. She might not be a proper grown-up teacher, but it couldn't be that hard to teach someone how to read and write, could it?

She'd gone to bed with her head full of ideas. She ignored the news update on television about Toby, secure in the knowledge that he was safe and well.

Next morning, she packed some food into her satchel and carefully chose a couple of writing books she'd used back in Year Four. On the way to school, she popped into the corner shop to ask about proper fuel for a lamp, telling yet another white lie that she was going camping, and bought a small bottle of pinkish liquid called methylated spirit.

Arriving at school early, she made her way to the boiler room entrance and, half way down the steps, stopped in disbelief.

There on the door was a bright, new silver padlock.

"Oh, no!"

She went down and pushed the door, but it was firmly shut.

The caretaker must have been down the night before and repaired what should have been repaired days earlier. 'Oh, why couldn't he have waited just a few days longer?' Sally muttered to herself.

She felt a great temptation to bash the door down, to beat it until it broke, but that would have been futile.

What on Earth could she do?

"Think," she whispered to herself. "Think!"

What she didn't want was to be caught hanging around the staircase, so she came out and sat on a bench in the playground. Teachers began to arrive at school and without fail commented how early she was and wasn't she cold sitting there?

No miss. No sir. A bit, miss.

Mr Jarvis arrived.

"Hello, Sally! Have you been sleeping here all night?" he joked.

"No, sir," she said, taking him seriously.

"What are you doing?"

"Just waiting."

"What for?"

"School, sir."

"Go in the hall and wait, Sally. If anyone asks, tell them I sent you because you look blue with cold. Alright?"

"Thank you, sir."

"And don't come so early tomorrow."

"No, sir."

Sally sat in the hall and warmed up a bit next to the radiator. What a stupid thing! What an impossible thing! She wanted to throw everything through the window and scream and cry and just give up. But she didn't. In fact, as she looked around in anger and despair at everything, she started to think.

Toby was getting in and out of his hidey-hole in different ways, not just the door which was now locked. So, if he could get out, she could get in!

She tried to remember the maze of rooms and the layout of the passages beyond the hatch and up the stairs. Where did it all lead to? It certainly didn't lead into the classrooms or the corridors. But it had to be somewhere the cleaners worked because she'd heard them. Where was the most likely place to give access to that downstairs lair?

Trying to keep the map of the school in her head, there really seemed to be only one possible other exit, and she was sitting in it – the hall! And in the hall there was only one possibility, and that was the stage.

The stage!

She'd been in school plays and remembered the

wings and stairs behind it. There were doors, she recalled, to storage rooms and who knew what. There had to be a connecting route, somewhere, somehow, and she had to find it.

Making sure no one was around, Sally climbed onto the stage and crept behind the curtains into the wings. At the rear of the right wing was a staircase, barred by a small wooden gate. The gate was only there as a precaution against falling so Sally opened it and walked down. At the bottom was a corridor with a door at the other side and a door half way along. She guessed that the door at the far side led to a staircase up to the other wing, so she left it and went to the middle one. It was open. This was only half a surprise because if it was the one Toby used, it would have to be open. Inside it was pitch black. She found the light switch, flicked it on and closed the door.

The room was large, full of old props and materials from past school productions. There were nooks and crannies and separate recesses, all full of dusty boxes.

"Toby?"

Sally called half in a whisper, half aloud.

"Toby, it's me."

No answer.

"Toby, I'm here. They've locked the door. I can't get in and I'm here but I don't know where the entrance is. Toby?"

Nothing.

Sally searched around, looking for a clear space

where a trapdoor to the basement might be found. The store room was actually three areas, some of them opening into quite large shelved spaces. In the second one she saw a small brass ring embedded into the floor!

Sally crept closer to it and knocked twice, then whispered, "Toby? It's me. Come on, it's Sally. Open up!"

From below there came a muffled sound of haste and panic.

The trapdoor stayed shut.

Sally put her finger in the ring and pulled.

It was locked!

"Not again!"

From her side there was no bolt. Perhaps it was only stuck. She pulled again.

No luck.

Angry, Sally pulled once more as hard as she could.

The trapdoor opened suddenly, and she fell backwards with surprise.

When she sat up, she saw Toby's head poking out. He was staring at her, bewildered.

Nothing

"What you doing here?" asked the disembodied head.

"The boiler room door's locked," Sally almost shouted in relief. "The caretaker's put a new padlock on it. I couldn't get in. Mr Jarvis sent me to the hall and I remembered what you said and I tried to find the trapdoor and when I did it was shut so I pulled and fell over. It just opened suddenly."

"There's a bolt on the other side," said Toby. "I opened it just now. I thought you weren't going to come. Quick!"

Sally turned off the light, crept to the hole and climbed down the ladder Toby had set up, into the darkness below. When she was down, Toby closed the trapdoor and bolted it shut.

"I'm so relieved," said Sally. "I thought I wouldn't get to see you and you'd think I'd told the police or something."

"Nah, I believe you now."

"I've brought lots of things," said Sally. "Look."

She took out the food, the books and the methylated spirit for the lamp.

"Let's light it now," said Toby. "This torch is

going up the spout again."

"But it's got new batteries," said Sally.

"I used it a lot last night," said Toby. "I worked till me eyes nearly dropped out. Let's do the lamp."

Together, they filled it, set it on a level place away from anything that might catch fire then struck a match to light the wick. It caught in a moment and they fitted the glass canopy snug over the flame which soon settled to a gentle blue light.

"It's really pretty," said Sally.

Toby didn't answer but sat, like Sally, staring at the beautiful flame. Torch light was less friendly and less warming. This was a kind, even glow which made them both feel more at ease. Even so, Sally said, "I do wish you'd come out, Toby. I was thinking, you could stay with me. Mum and dad wouldn't mind. They might let us come back down here when we felt like it, for fun, like camping. It's just that doing it without them knowing, and them all thinking that you're missing and, maybe, well, dead, I mean that's what most of them think anyway, it's not fair, is it?"

"Don't care."

This irritated Sally because he ought to care. She did, other people did, so he should, too. But on the other hand, she told herself, he wasn't quite right yet, so she had to be patient with him and didn't tell him off. She also didn't want to give him reasons to call her bossy again.

"Can I show you what I done?" he asked.

"Something clever?"

"You tell me. You're the teacher."

Toby took out his writing books. Overnight he had filled up a complete book with the patterns she had shown him. They started off quite neat, but as they went on they became more and more untidy until at the end they were unreadable.

"I got tired at the end," he said.

"They're good at the beginning," said Sally, "really good. I couldn't do them as nice as that."

"Really?"

"Almost really. But you get messy. Look. I can't read these."

"But I wanted to finish the book."

"You didn't have to. What counts is doing it properly. There's no point in doing it if you don't do it properly."

"I knew you wouldn't like it."

"I do like it. I said so. But you did too much. How long did this take you?"

"Don't know. Hours."

"Didn't you sleep?"

"Bit. Went out into the hall at three o'clock in the morning. Got the apparatus out and did P.E."

"You didn't?"

"I did. Got the ropes out and climbed up and down them like anything."

"Toby, you're mad!"

"I know."

"What if you had an accident?"

"I put a mat there."

"But still, that's dangerous!"

"Don't care. It was fun. I was all alone. No teacher to say, 'Don't do this, don't do that'. It was great."

"One day the cleaners will come in the morning and find you on the floor with a broken leg."

"Don't care."

"You keep saying that, but I bet you do care, about some things."

"No, I don't. I don't care about nuffing."

"It's 'nothing'" said Sally, "not 'nuffing'. What about me?"

Toby shrugged.

"What have you got to do with anything?" he asked, rudely.

"Suppose I get caught? What will happen to me?"

"You'll be alright. They'll just tell you off. What else can they do?"

"But I don't want to be told off, not by people who like me. Worse, by people who love me."

"No one loves me, so it don't matter and I don't care."

Sally decided she and Toby could argue like this forever, bashing a tennis ball of an idea back and forth till the cows came home.

"Still think you do," she said, "inside. Anyway, I've brought you these things and this food."

Toby tucked into the food that Sally had brought and finished most of it quite quickly.

"Can you get some more?"

"You haven't finished this yet. And besides…"

Toby waited for Sally to say what 'besides' she meant. "You've forgotten something," she said. Toby couldn't think of anything he'd forgotten. "'Thank you'," Sally reminded him.

"Oh, okay. What books did you get?"

Sally raised her eyes to heaven, or at least to the low ceiling of the stale, dank and dark room she found herself in.

"You're a case," she said. "Do you know that?" He did. "I got these to read," said Sally, "and these to practise writing."

She handed him the writing books which he looked at with great attention. Sally noticed that Toby, when he concentrated on something, was far more intense about it than anyone else she knew; he really put all his mind into what he was doing.

"Are they too hard?" she asked.

"No. Just letters and more patterns. I can do them by tonight. Can you get me Book Two?"

"Do Book One first and then I'll bring Book Two. There's no point hurrying. If you rush and do it all wrong, you'll have to do it all over again. Have you got enough pencils?"

Toby showed her the pencils he'd taken from the stock room. Sally shook her head, despairing at such lack of conscience.

"I'll show you a few letters," she said.

She took the book and set to work. Toby watched her, fascinated.

"These are capital letters," she told him. "You know what that means?"

"Course I do."

"What?"

"I just do," Toby said, evasively. "Don't have to tell you."

"They're for beginnings of sentences and names of people and places," said Sally, seeing that he didn't have a clue. "Do them today and you can do small letters tomorrow. Maybe numbers the next day. That's if you don't come out of this grubby little hole first," she added turning her nose up at their musty, dusty classroom.

"I won't," whispered Toby who had already begun to copy Sally's letters. She watched him, fascinated. He held the pencil like a baby until she twisted it in his hand to hold it properly. His eyes were fixed like laser beams on the paper. Sally couldn't remember once in class that she'd seen him so focused.

"I've got to go now," she said,

"Alright."

"See you."

"Alright."

"If the beast doesn't eat you first."

"Alright."

Sally shook her head again. She could have said anything and Toby would have replied, 'Alright.' She put her hand on his shoulder and said, "You're a good boy really, Toby."

Something registered in Toby's mind and he stopped writing.

"What?"

"'Pardon,'" Sally corrected him. "I said you're a good boy Toby, deep down. And you're probably quite clever."

"You reckon?"

"I do. I have to go now, though. Are you going to let me out?"

Toby studied Sally as if she was somehow different from the clever clogs he always thought she was, then he unbolted the trapdoor and let her out.

"I hope I'm not late for school," she said. "What if there's people in the hall?"

"Wait till they go. No one will know where you've been."

Oddly, Sally didn't want to go. It was dark and gloomy and cold, but there was more meaning down here with sad little Toby than there was upstairs where the sun shone. She couldn't understand this at all.

"Bring me somefing else tonight," said Toby. That snapped her out of her dream. "I need a blanket," said Toby. "To keep me warm."

"Toby," Sally pleaded for one last time. "Won't you let me tell someone? Then you can come out and have as many blankets as you like. Forever."

"It don't work like that," said Toby, wisely.

"You can change your mind, you know, any time."

"Bring me the blanket?"

"I'll try. And watch the lamp. It's dangerous, you know. Don't knock it over."

"Bossy boots."

"Must go. See you later. Bye."

"Bye."

Over

Sally made her way out by the light of the lamp which shone through the trapdoor opening. As she left the room, she could see Toby's sad round eyes staring after her like the glass button eyes of a teddy bear. She couldn't be sure, but she thought there was something more he wanted to say as he watched her leave, but he said nothing. Perhaps he didn't like her very much; she wouldn't blame him for that. What she never guessed, though, was how desperate he'd become. Once again, after such a short a visit, his single friend and contact with the world was leaving and once again he'd found it impossible to say the right things to her. Toby was used only to mistreatment and believed that was the way everyone behaved. Reluctant to let her go, he waited until Sally had disappeared completely before bolting the trapdoor shut and imprisoning himself in the loneliness and gloom.

At school, time seemed to pass at a snail's pace. Sally's mind kept straying back to the peculiar boy locked away in the belly of the school, like Jonah in the whale. She was distracted and impatient but also determined to keep the secret. She also felt quite grown up. It hadn't been easy making the move from junior school to secondary school. Sometimes she felt that she was still in the cosy comfort of a homely little group of classrooms, forgetting that she was now growing up, with all that entailed. If what she'd discovered didn't make her grow up good and proper now, nothing would.

After her English lesson, Mr Jarvis did just what Sally hoped he wouldn't do and asked her to speak with him.

"Is everything alright, Sally?"

"Yes, sir."

"You've been very different these past few days. I wondered whether anyone has been bothering you?"

"No, sir."

"Not Jonas? He hasn't bullied you at all?"

"No, sir."

"If he does, or anyone does, you must tell someone straight away."

"I will, sir."

"What time did you go to bed last night?"

"Early, sir. About ten o'clock."

"You look tired. Would you like me to ask your mum and dad to come to school? If there's something worrying you we could talk about it together."

"Oh, no, sir! I'm alright. Honest."

"Well you don't look it. And to get to school so early is unnecessary. You can't help but be tired during the day."

"I like getting here early," Sally heard herself lying and wondered where the lie was coming from.

"Hmm," said Mr Jarvis, still suspecting that Sally was hiding something, "but remember, if you're worried about work or this business with Toby, you let your parents or the school know. I'm sure you'd do that anyway. Don't keep things all to yourself."

"Everyone has secrets, though, sir, don't they?"

She couldn't believe she'd said that, but she had.

"Yes. I suppose they do," Mr Jarvis admitted. It was sometimes so hard to teach children lessons; they seemed to know so much already. "But there are secrets and secrets. No one can tell you what you should keep to yourself and what you should share, you have to judge that for yourself. You're a wise girl. You'll know."

Sally wondered if that was true. She wasn't keeping the kind of secret Mr Jarvis had in mind, but a much more serious one, one that she really didn't know what to do with for the best. The main thing, she thought, was that she had given her promise and she would never forgive herself if she broke her word. She would have loved to ask Mr Jarvis what to do and was oh so temptingly close to doing so. It would have been terribly easy and perhaps right as well, but she kept quiet and her teacher said, "Don't forget, if there is anything or anyone bothering you, tell your parents. They'll help, and so will we."

In the playground, Michelle and Jackie were bursting to know what was going on. They knew 'something was up, as you do with friends who are behaving a little oddly. They asked Sally a heap of questions but got irritated when she didn't give them a straight answer. Sally was puzzled because she'd done her best to act normal, but it felt like everyone, teachers, parents and friends knew something was amiss, as if they could see inside her head, which was scary.

None of them came close to guessing though. It was too strange a situation, but she carried Toby with her wherever she went and he must have affected the way she looked, the way she spoke and the way she behaved in every way. You couldn't keep a secret like that and expect people not to notice something a bit odd about you.

The talk came back to Toby and there was no way Sally could change the subject. The missing boy was a magnet for every conversation and it naturally made Sally more uncomfortable than ever.

"Did you hear anything on the news today?" asked Jackie.

"Same," said Michelle, "nothing new. It's been over a week now. How's he going to live?"

"Dunno," said Jackie. "Maybe he robs places. He's a bit of a magpie. I'd rob too if it was that or starve."

"Would you?" asked Sally. "Is it right to?"

"If it's thieve or die, I'd thieve," said Jackie. "Wouldn't you two?"

Michelle said she never would. Sally turned a faint shade of pink.

"Perhaps he's living in a cave by the sea," said Jackie, "far away. What do you think, Sal?"

"Maybe."

"Or in a forest somewhere. Perhaps he's gone abroad to the Amazon Rain Forest and is living there."

"Don't be silly," said Michelle.

"I'm not. I reckon Toby could get anywhere he wanted. As long as he's alright I don't care what he does."

"Me neither," said Michelle. "If he comes back – when he comes back – we'll be good to him. All of us."

Sally didn't say a word. She just determined to persuade Toby to change his mind right away and come out. She couldn't carry on like this for many more moments, let alone days and even weeks. Impossible!

"You're not saying much, Sal," observed Michelle.

"Tired," said Sally.

"It's got to be over soon," said Jackie. "Something bad will happen if they don't catch him."

"Something bad might already have happened," said Michelle.

"No," said Sally, "it won't be over badly, you mustn't think that!"

Her friends looked at her as if they were trying to read her mind, like grown-ups.

"Can't help thinking it," said Michelle.

"Everyone's saying it. It's obvious, isn't it? That's what they're saying on the news all the time, that's what…"

"No!" said Sally. "If you go on about it being over in a bad way, you'll make it bad."

"What, like your stories?"

"My stories are stupid!" said Sally, which really made them blink. "They don't come true and it was silly to believe it. There's no beast, never was and never will be."

"Well you didn't think that when you went hunting for it," said Jackie. "What changed your mind?"

Sally didn't answer, not wanting to get into an awkward argument. The whole thing was already awkward beyond measure. The only thing she wanted and her friends and the rest of the world wanted was it to be over with a happy ending, but whereas they all thought that the boy was in serious trouble, she knew that it wasn't Toby who would be in trouble, it was her, the little liar Sally Shakespeare.

Pencil

"I won't!" said Toby.

"But why not?" Sally said, hands on hips and hot under the collar. It had been a long day, full of questions from home and school, and she'd been nervous dodging behind the stage without being seen. She'd had to walk through the hall three times before the opportunity arose, and she headed down into the forgotten space beneath the school.

Once there, she'd set her mind on persuading Toby to see reason and come out, and she really thought that she could do it, but Toby thought otherwise. They were both stubborn as mules.

"Because I don't want to!"

"I, I, I!" mocked Sally. "Don't you ever think of anyone else?"

"They don't fink of me."

"They do! What have I just been telling you? Everyone's on about you all day long."

Toby still had no idea that the entire nation was waiting for news about him. His world was his mum and dad, and they didn't seem to care about him too much, nor school where everyone laughed at him or bullied him, so it didn't make sense that just because he was missing everyone was suddenly shedding tears. Not to mention the fact that he was quite enjoying himself for the strange reason that he had a friend at last, and who was it but the class clever clogs Sally Shakespeare. But he wouldn't tell her that, ever.

"No they ain't," he said. "You're just making that up."

Sally took a deep breath and breathed out.

"You're impossible, Toby. I ought to go, you know, and leave you down here all by yourself."

"I didn't ask you to come," he said in reply. "You can go if you want," he added, taking the chance that she might truly get fed up and leave him. For some reason, though, he didn't think she would. "They don't care," said Toby, sulkily. "They'd be the same if anyone had gone missing. Even Jonas."

"That's not the point," insisted Sally. "You're missing and they can't think of anything else. Not just them. All the kids in the school. All the teachers, too. And the mums and dads. Everywhere."

"Don't care."

"You keep saying that, but it's not an answer Toby, and I don't believe you anyway."

"If I come out," he said, "it'll be just the same as before. Do this, Toby, don't do that, Toby, ha, ha, ha, whack, whack, whack. I hate them."

"It might be different now," Sally said more softly. "Your mum and dad won't be able to do what they did any more. Not now people know about it."

"Too late," said Toby. "I don't like them. Don't

like school, never will. Might be different for a day or two, but it'll be just the same in the end."

Sally felt oddly out-argued, as if there was more truth in what Toby was saying than what she was saying. She could argue till she was blue in the face, but he might be right after all. Things might change for a while, then it would all be back to normal again. How could she or he change things forever? It seemed awfully hard.

"Well what do you expect?" she said petulantly but with a hint of intuition. "You want to be looked at all the time, don't you? You want to be made a fuss of?"

"No, I don't."

"Yes, you do. That's why you muck about so much."

"No it ain't! And I don't muck about. I don't care if no one looks at me!"

He was irritated because what Sally had said rang bells.

"Bet you do."

"Don't. Anyway, if all you've come down here to do is tell me off, you might as well go. You're just the same as the rest of them."

Sally flushed with anger and frustration, uncertain what to do for the best. She half wanted to stalk off in a huff and leave him there on his lonesome grumpy self, but she wanted more to help him and so she said in as grown up a way as possible, "Let's argue later, Toby. Did you do any writing?"

"Bit."

Toby perked up a little and showed Sally his book.

"You've done about ten pages!"

"Don't take long."

"Doesn't take long," corrected Sally, letting the teacher role go to her head a little.

"That's what I said. What's it like?"

Toby had written capital letters over and over again.

"It's alright Toby," Sally said, surprised. "It's more than alright; it's good."

"Watch," he said, and he began to write faster and neater than Sally dared hope. It wasn't anywhere near the speed and neatness of most of the other children in the class, but it was much better than it had been before.

"That's brilliant!" she said. "You're quite smart, Toby. Shall we do some more?"

"Course," he said. "If you think I'm getting better."

"Much better. Honest. Look, these are the small letters."

She showed him the lower case alphabet in the second part of the book.

"What you have to do," she went on, "is copy them one at a time till you get good, then join them up with the bits on the end. I'll show you."

Sally took a pencil and wrote out the letters of the alphabet with their hooks and showed Toby how they joined up.

"Don't try joining them till you can do them all separately."

"I won't. Let me try."

He took the pencil and began to write a few letters. Sally watched him, fascinated at how hard he concentrated. She thought he was going to break the pencil, he held it so hard and tight. She showed him how to hold it properly and he listened so attentively it made her feel like a real teacher. She wondered whether there was something wrong with Toby's fingers because they seemed to slip back into holding the pencil like a tennis racquet, but he never threw a tantrum or said he couldn't do it, like he did in class. He tried until he held it lightly but firmly.

"It feels weird," he said.

"That's because you're not used to it," said Sally feeling very wise and knowledgeable. "The more you do it, the easier it gets. You just do it without thinking. I do, anyway."

"That's 'cos you're a genius," said Toby.

"It's just writing," said Sally, modestly. "Don't press too hard, that's right. Try to see the letter in your head before you write it."

Toby managed to break three pencil tips before getting the hang of it and writing without ripping holes in the paper. He followed the patterns and seemed happy to write single letters over and over again. Sally wondered whether he would write the letter 'a' for the rest of his life if she let him. It seemed to calm him down, knowing what to do and finding it easier with every passing moment. Sally was beginning to think that it was all so easy and that she had the knack of teaching when Toby looked up and said, "I've had enough of this. What else did you bring me?"

Queen

"Nothing," said Sally, taken aback, "because you're so rude."

"I ain't."

"You are, Toby. You're the rudest boy on the planet, but you can't help it, can you?"

He didn't answer. He wondered if she meant it, then smiled in a surprisingly nice way. Sally delved into her bag.

"I've got this," she said. "My mum made it for the dog but he isn't using it."

"For the dog?" Toby was offended.

"Well I can't bring our best stuff, can I?" Sally told him. "What would they say?"

She took out a funny little blanket knitted together from patches of many different colours. Toby held it up to inspect it. He seemed pleased.

"Is it alright, then?" asked Sally.

"Yeh, it's alright," Toby answered.

"Will you be comfortable in it?"

"I'll be a bug in a rug," Toby said, and they both laughed.

Toby laid the blanket down and curled up in it. Sally stared at him and said, "There was a bug who lived in a rug..." and waited for him to catch on. Toby stared back, his brain working at a hundred miles an hour.

"He had a very ugly mug..." he said.

"So he hid away in a dark little hole..." said Sally.

"And didn't come out till he was old," said Toby. "The End."

Sally looked at him, all curled up and being suddenly clever with words.

"That's quite hard to do," she said.

Toby didn't answer, just pointed to his mouth with a plaintive expression. Sally delved into her bag again and took out some bread and cheese, raisins, scones, chocolate bars, a couple of tins of drink and some tea bags. Toby looked at it all but said nothing. He snuck into his own bag and took out a tin of beans and an egg.

"I took these from the kitchen," he said, "so it's not real stealing. You said it wasn't."

Sally couldn't remember whether she'd said this or not, but the fact was that Toby had to eat, and to a certain extent rules and regulations had to go out of the window in this kind of emergency. She never thought she'd think such a thing, but she was thinking it now.

"How are you going to make them?" she asked.

Toby said, "I've got this. I didn't show it to you because I really need it and you mustn't take it away."

He brought out a small gas burning stove.

Sally shook her head. Taking an egg or two from the kitchen was one thing; stealing expensive cooking equipment from a shop was another, emergency or not. Besides, this emergency was self-inflicted.

"Toby!"

"I need it," he said. "If you don't let me keep it, I won't have nuffing hot to eat."

"Toby, it's not right, none of this. I know you have to eat and drink, and you can break a few rules to do that, I suppose, but why don't you just come out with me. Everything will be alright. They're not going to put you in prison. You won't have to steal any more, either."

Toby became a touch ratty.

"It ain't the worst thing in the world, you know. I haven't murdered anyone or stolen the Crown Jewels. It's only a little stove. Why d'you have to make such a fuss? You're like the queen, you are, bossing everyone around."

Sally couldn't help herself and started laughing.

"I wish I was the queen," she said. "I'd have a crown and everything."

Toby ignored her, set the stove up and lit the flame. He adjusted it with the small knob until it burned a gentle blue colour. Sally watched him, astonished at how deft he was. She couldn't do that, but he was handling it all like a trained boy scout. Then he took out a saucepan and her admiration turned to desperation.

"It's filthy!" she exclaimed, horrified.

"I was going to wash it."

"When, Toby? You'll die if you eat from that."

"No I won't."

"Well, you'll get ill. Is it stolen?"

"Nah. I found it. Where's the beans?"

Sally couldn't work him out. One moment he was sensible and focused, the next he was eating from a grubby pan that looked as if it harboured every disease under the sun. Sally scrubbed it out as best she could with some wire wool and cloth, but it still looked suspiciously foul. Toby opened the tin of beans with a rusty old tin opener and poured the beans into the saucepan. Then he cracked the egg and dropped it into the beans. Sally watched him, fascinated. She'd never done anything like that, so she had to hand it to him, he was a bit of a clever clogs himself.

Soon, the makeshift meal began to heat up and steam started to spread from the pan.

"I reckon this'll be empty, soon," said Toby.

"What will?"

"The gas. Can you get me another one?"

"Not if you want me to steal it," she said. "How much are they?"

Toby didn't know. He'd never bought much in his life. His parents didn't give him pocket money so he hadn't a clue as to the cost of anything.

Sally watched him stir his meal with a kitchen spoon and again saw that wonderful concentration on his face. At that moment she would have liked to buy him a hundred gas cartridges.

She sniffed the aroma from the egg and baked beans.

"That's nice," she said.

"Course it is. I'm a good cooker."

"Cook," she corrected. "What else have you made?"

"Not that much. Mainly beans because there's so many of them in the kitchen."

"Don't you get really hungry, Toby?"

"Same as I eat at home, this is."

"Egg and beans? All the time?"

"Not all the time, but a lot. It's almost ready."

He took out a plate which also hadn't been washed, and dished out his meal.

"Want some?" he asked.

"No, thanks. You eat it. I'll have supper when I get home."

Toby ate in silence, enjoying the meal and the praise he got from Sally. When he had finished, he asked her, "Does your mum make nice meals?"

"And my dad. They're both good cooks."

"What you having tonight?"

"Don't know. Maybe Stew. Meat in gravy, carrots, peas, potatoes, bits of onions. Something like that."

"D'you have puddings and things?"

"Rhubarb pie."

"Can you save me a bit?"

"A bit of pie?"

"Yes."

"I'll try."

"You can do it. You're clever, you are. Bet you had to lie a bit to do all this."

Sally went red with shame. She had no answer.

"See," said Toby. "You have to do wrong things sometimes."

"I don't like it though."

"You'll get used to it in a while."

"That's just like you, Toby, it's so easy isn't it to lie and steal and make up good reasons for it all? I won't get used to it."

Toby bowed his head and listened, then said, "Bet you will."

"Won't. And if you say so again, I'm going. Really this time. You're the clever clogs, Toby Tinker, not me. You think you can get me to do anything you want. I don't have to do any of this. It's only because I like you that I do. You shouldn't make me feel bad, Toby, you shouldn't!"

Sally fought back tears and then it was Toby's turn to go red with shame. She'd said she liked him. That was the first time anyone had said that to him in his life, ever, ever and ever.

"I didn't mean it, Sally. Sorry. I say dumb things at times, but I don't mean them."

"Well don't say that again. You make me feel like a criminal."

"No, you're not. You'll never be one. I will, but you won't."

"You don't know what you're going to be," said Sally. "How do you know you're going to be a criminal?"

"I just do. I keep doing wrong things and they don't matter to me, but they matter to everyone else. I get told off for things all the time. I don't know what's right and what's wrong."

"Everyone knows that."

"I don't."

"Well, I'll teach you. For a start this is wrong."

"What?"

"Doing what you're doing."

"See, I told you."

"Told me what?"

"That you're bossy, like the queen."

"Well this *is* wrong, and because it's wrong you're making me do wrong things too. One wrong makes others, like waves in water."

"I like that," said Toby, missing the point entirely.

"You're not supposed to like it, you're supposed to understand it."

"I do, but I can't help it. It's me."

"That's not an excuse, Toby. I bet you've never tried."

"I have, and I always get told off, whatever I do."

"That's still no reason for lying and stealing. What would the world be like if everyone did that?"

"They do."

"Toby!"

"It's true. My dad says so."

"What, that everyone lies and steals?"

"Yeh. And if you don't do it too, you'll get lied

to and stolen from. That's what he says to me."

"Well he's wrong."

"How do you know? You're just a kid. He's grown up. He knows."

"Grown-ups don't know everything."

Sally was going to say, 'Especially your dad,' but she changed her mind and kept quiet. She was shocked to hear her own words, her, Sally Shakespeare, goody-goody brainbox who never put a foot wrong, doubting her parents, her teachers, the police, everyone!

After all, if grown-ups didn't know everything, who did?

Reading

Over the next few days, Sally became more expert at sneaking into the hall and behind the stage, down to Toby's hideaway. She came at all times of day, and even at the weekend when the school was open for clubs and community activities. Sometimes she nipped down for ten minutes, other times for an hour, but rarely longer. She didn't want anyone to notice she was missing, but of course they did, only not for long so this didn't raise suspicions.

She and Toby turned their minds to reading, something Toby had never mastered. She brought down some sound cards which no one used any more, not in the higher classes, anyway. They had letters printed on them like 'a' for apple with a picture of an apple, just in case you weren't sure what 'apple' meant, which Toby wasn't. He wasn't sure what anything meant and it was a great help having brainbox Sally there to help him. She told him everything he wanted to know but had been afraid to ask. He knew everyone thought he was stupid, and he believed it himself, but Sally was moving him along a good few miles an hour and he became a little more confident every day. He could recognise vowels and consonants and something that Sally called dipthongs, even though neither of them knew what that meant; it was just such a great word to say.

"It isn't as hard as I thought," he said.

She brought down some simple reading books about pirates and asked him to read a line, two lines, a paragraph, or even a page. Not everything Toby had been taught in ten years had gone in one ear and out the other. He remembered a few things and quite a lot was stuck in his brain but not finding its way out. Sally was as patient as Job and quite chuffed when she arrived each day to find her pupil busy at the homework she'd given him. It wasn't long before the language block started to lift and Toby started to see a little light at the end of a ten year long tunnel.

This was quite something and would have given some clever adults plenty of food for thought, but to the two of them it was quite natural. One of them was bright as a button, the other locked in a dark room, so it was only fair that one should help the other.

Sally found all kinds of things to bring him and ways to teach him. Some of it was taken from the lower years, even Years 3 and 4 which could have been embarrassing, but it was for a good cause, she decided. So, little bricks and little bath books found their way to Toby's Den, as they thought of it, along with bits and bobs a child of four would find interesting. Toby would have been shamed if he'd had to do this in front of others, but because he was alone with Sally and no one else could see, he didn't mind.

When he was alone, he studied hard and soon managed to read a complete pirate book. It was the earliest one in the series, but still difficult for someone who'd never read a word before. Hours flew by, and he made himself tired reading every sound and every word, remembering what his unusual teacher had taught him.

She was bossy, but he didn't mind. He quite liked the bossiness because it came with a lot of things he wanted to know and had never learned. In two weeks, he'd done more than he'd done in five years at school, although strictly speaking he was still there, just underneath it.

What mattered was that he was learning, and this was an amazing feeling! He began to feel much less stupid. He pulled fewer faces, made fewer weird noises and started to think a little like the other children in school must have felt.

At least, that's what he hoped.

He couldn't be sure because this was a funny situation with no one else apart from Sally around, but he felt certain that he was more like everyone else now that he could read the alphabet and make out a fair number of words.

The moments when Sally read to him were the most precious of all. He wasn't sure why, but he loved listening to all the different tales she told him. Some she made up on the spot, which was unbelievable. They arranged things very formally, just as if they were back in junior school.

"You sit down there," she said to Toby. "I'll sit on this old rusty stool which will be teacher's chair. Everyone be quiet now."

"Please, miss?"

"What do you want Toby?"

"You're a good teacher, Miss."

"I haven't taught you anything yet."

"Yes you have. You're teaching me reading and writing. I couldn't do that before."

"You keep trying hard," Sally said in her best teacher's voice, "and I'm sure you can be as good as anyone else in the class. Now I'll begin."

If any adults could have witnessed these scenes, they would have been struck by the picture of the two children playing their parts so wonderfully well. Each became fully engrossed in the role they were acting out and performed it to perfection. A stillness surrounded them which made their troubles seem distant, and all that counted and all that was true was the reading, the story and the gentle glow of the lamp.

Spelling

Another few days passed and the world started to mourn the lost Toby, even though he was right there under the noses of his teachers, learning faster and better than he'd ever learned before.

"Alright," said Sally, "we'll start on spelling."

She'd thought about this and decided it was important for Toby to learn how to spell. Her parents had helped her learn to spell when she was only four years old and she could tackle long words like 'beautiful' and 'colourful' without putting double letters where they weren't wanted or missing out the odd vowel if they didn't seem necessary. She also knew how to use apostrophes, which was a dying art amongst grown-ups let alone classrooms. She was determined to be strict with Toby because he would appreciate it later on in life, as her father had told her many years earlier when she was being obstreperous for some reason.

"Ready?"

"Yep."

"Number one, 'book'."

Toby wrote 'duk'.

"Number two, 'doll'."

Toby wrote 'dul'.

"Number three, 'friend'."

Toby wrote 'frend'.

Sally called out twenty words. Toby wrote them down and then they marked them together.

"They're all wrong, Toby."

"I can see that."

"Why?"

"Because I can't spell," he said, as if it was a silly question.

"But why, Toby? Can't you hear the sounds?"

Toby was sullen. He had done a lot of work the night before on joined up handwriting and he was beginning to feel a little more confident. Now he was feeling thick as a brick again and realised how far he still had to go.

"Can't we do something else," he said in a fake bright voice.

"No, we can't. What's the point of writing if you can only write rubbish? You have to learn these words."

"I can't, not just like that."

"Well how else are you going to learn them?"

"I need time."

"You haven't got time."

"What's the day today?"

"What difference does that make?"

"When do I have to learn them by?"

"Yesterday," said Sally, getting irritated with her pupil.

"What's the point of me learning words for no

reason?"

"There is a reason."

"What?"

"Well..."

"Well?"

"Because the next twenty will be a tiny bit easier, and the next will be a tiny bit easier still and so on until you can spell millions of words easily. Besides," said Sally, "when you come to think about it, if you can't spell, you might as well be a monkey or a chimpanzee, and you're not, you're human. You're the only animal that can write."

Toby was going to object to being called an animal, but Sally went on.

"No other animal can do what we do, even what you do, Toby. No animal can hold a pencil..."

"Neither can I."

"You can now."

"But I'll never write clever stuff like you, never. What's the point?"

Sally found it hard to explain. It was something she knew was important and Toby ought to know it too. They were wasting time discussing it, and they were only discussing it because Toby found it too hard. He was using what Captain Kirk would have called 'Evasive Tactics.'

"You will write like me," said Sally, "or rather, you will write like you. We all write in different ways, but we spell the same. If we don't, we won't be able to understand each other. We'll be like cavemen again."

"Ugh!" said Toby.

"Look," said Sally. "We can do it like we do reading, only backwards. Listen to these sounds... oo... ee... bl... sm..."

"What are you talking about?"

"They're bits of words. You need sounds to make up words. It isn't rocket science Toby," she said, even though to Toby it was probably a lot harder than rocket science.

"See," said Sally. "If you know letter sounds, you'll be able to write whole words. I'll teach you the sounds and you can learn thirty words a day."

"You said twenty."

"Well you've got loads of time. You can even learn forty."

"Forty!"

"Why not? Make it fifty."

"I can't learn fifty words in a day!"

"Course you can. And, let's see, ten sounds."

"Fifty words and ten sounds!"

"You have to learn them and write them. I'll test you and you mustn't make a mistake."

"What happens if I do? Will you tell me off like a real teacher? Otherwise I won't bother."

"That's up to you. I thought you wanted to learn."

"I do."

"Well if you don't do what I want, the punishment will be you'll stay illegitimate for ever," said Sally, trying to be really clever and mixing up her long words.

"What's that? 'Ill and giti mate'?"

"It means you'll be ignorant and people won't respect you. They'll just laugh at you."

"They laugh at me anyway. When I'm bigger, I'll hit them."

"Toby!"

Toby went sullen again.

"Go on then," he said, rethinking the future, "tell me which words you want me to learn."

Sally picked out the words from a book of spelling lists she'd brought with her and marked off fifty.

"Those," she said, "and here are some sounds, too," and she wrote down some sounds she remembered: "'ee' and 'ea'.'"

"How do you know the difference?" asked Toby.

"What do you mean?"

"Between 'ee' and 'ea' and any uver 'eeee'?" Toby asked.

"You just do. Practise," and she wrote down some more sounds, speaking them as she wrote, "'sm', 'bl', 'cl', 'fl', 'gr', 'sr'"

"What's 'sr'?" asked Toby. "I don't know any words with 'sr'."

Sally thought, but couldn't come up with one either.

"You're a dumb teacher," said Toby.

"That shows you're clever," said Sally. "You don't just do what I tell you, you think about it. That's good."

She crossed out the 'sr' and wrote another sound

instead. They seemed to go on forever, and she wondered how she'd ever managed to learn them all herself.

"What you also have to do," she said, "is write down three words for each sound. Can you do that?"

"Dunno. This is loads of work, miss."

"I'm not 'miss', I'm just me," said Sally, "but I like being a teacher."

"That's 'cos you're bossy anyway."

Despite his complaints, he set to work and didn't take any notice when she slipped out, back into the real world. If Mr Jarvis had seen how committed Toby was, how hard he worked and how focused he'd become, he might have given up teaching and taken up a less difficult job, like being Prime Minister. It was a remarkable turnaround, the problem boy becoming in just a few days a model student, even if it was alone in the dark, damp and cold in the belly of a school where everyone believed they would never, ever see him again.

Time

It was almost three weeks before Sally realised that Toby couldn't tell the time. When she found out, she didn't know what to say. It was something everybody learned when they crawled out of prams, but Toby had missed out on this, just as he'd missed out on everything else to do with learning. No wonder he was so restless and silly in class. He wanted the others to know he was in trouble but didn't know how to ask. Sally felt real pity for him, which didn't stop her from being strict, telling him he had no choice, he had to learn the time *now*, and she emphasised the word as if the world would come to an end if he didn't do it.

She smuggled down a toy clock, one that you could push the hands around, with giant numbers and deep black lines for each minute of the hour. As with reading and writing, for Sally it was second nature. She'd learned all this stuff when she was little, even before she came to school, and didn't think twice about it. If you thought twice about every word you wrote and read, and every moment you looked at a clock or a watch, then you'd never get anywhere, or maybe you would, but very slowly.

She didn't talk to Toby like he was a baby, because that would have upset him, but she realised that she had to take things at a snail's pace. She sat down beside him with the clock between them and showed him how the hands moved and the fact that one was bigger than the other. He didn't even know that.

"How did you get to school on time?" she asked him, puzzled to bits. How could he have done anything? But it turned out that Toby had found ways around his difficulties. He watched others and followed them, kept quiet when he didn't want to be noticed, and made a noise when he wanted to use evasive tactics, in other words to stop others really seeing his empty head.

It wasn't truly empty, it had all the pieces in it, like a jigsaw, but they were jumbled up, as if they hadn't been taken out of the box and sorted, let alone fitted together. He was a magician, in a way, doing tricks every day to get by, joining in with what others were doing at the time they were doing it, swimming like a fish alongside countless other fish, upstream or downstream, deflecting attention one minute, attracting it the next, but not for help, not truly, only to avoid being found out.

He went to bed when he was told or when he felt tired, not because he knew the time was nine or ten. Hours meant nothing to him. Nor did the seconds and minutes in between.

Sally explained how a day was divided into twenty-four hours.

"Why?" asked Toby, and asked the same thing for everything she said until she got fed up and told him to accept that this was the way time was counted. There might be an answer to 'why' but she wasn't clever enough to answer that. It just *was*! Toby nodded and counted to twenty-four to make sure he got that into his 'thick head' as he called it.

"It isn't thick," said Sally, "just muddled. I'll un-muddle you, Toby."

She did her level best to do this. She made him count to sixty to get the idea of seconds and minutes, then told him to imagine sixty of those minutes as an hour. Toby squeezed his eyes shut and Sally could almost hear his brain ticking over like a real watch. She moved the hand a minute forward.

"It ain't much, is it?" said Toby. Sally had to agree, a minute was a tiny movement, especially when counting to sixty seemed to take forever. So sixty of those minutes felt like eternity, and when they focused on it like that, it did.

Toby played with the hands of the clock, making sure he knew which was the big hand and which the small hand. He was thrown when Sally told him that there was also a second hand which moved quite quickly and didn't know what to say when Toby asked why they'd left it out, except to guess that the clock would become too crowded.

Toby had seen electronic times on a million things, but he hadn't made the connection between the numbers and a clock. This astonished Sally, but she patiently explained how the whole kit and caboodle worked, but even she came unstuck when Toby started asking questions about the Sun, the Earth and the moon and how this all fitted into the giant toy clock. It seemed to Sally that Toby was asking extremely difficult questions which someone who didn't think about things wouldn't ask. She promised to find out the answers to things she didn't know, but still said it would be better if he left his dumpy, lonely schoolroom and found out for himself. Toby grumbled a response but was unwilling to say he was enjoying clever Sally Shakespeare teaching him and didn't fancy returning to the light, bright world just yet.

He got to grips with hours, minutes and seconds and learned how to say the time, before the hour and past the hour, quarters, halves and any number of minutes in between. When Sally wasn't there, he stared at the clock and moved the minute hand around, one twitch at a time, from twelve midnight to twelve midday and back to twelve midnight, saying each time as if he was getting to know an old friend who he hadn't seen for ages. He even, quite wonderfully, worked out that there were one thousand, four hundred and forty minutes in a day. He did this in a long winded manner in his head, without using pencil and paper, ashamed that he didn't know how to write it out. That would be on his new list of "Fings To Lurn". He tried testing it by counting to sixty, one thousand four hundred and forty times, which should have meant he finished at exactly the same time the next day. Most normal people would have given up after a minute or two, but Toby wasn't normal and had no distractions. He decided that he quite liked the comfort of counting. There was something reassuring about the sheer regularity of it, as if beneath the many mysteries he didn't understand was something that he did. He told Sally how far he'd got and she was amazed. She didn't think she'd be able to count anywhere near so long.

Untidy

Sally had already tried to get some order in Toby's Den but it wasn't easy. The place had been a dump for all manner of rubbish and Toby hadn't cleared much of it out of the way, nor was he by nature or training an ordered boy.

"I can't do this alone. You'll have to help me," she said to him.

"I'm busy. I'm learning how to read and write," he answered, without looking up.

"You've got all day to do that. You have to tidy up. It's a pit in here. It's unhealthy." Toby grumbled something under his breath. "Toby, it's not right to live like this. You're a human being, not an animal."

"I think it's alright," he muttered. "Nuffing wrong with it."

"Yes, there is! Come on. We can do it together ."

Toby slowly looked up, stared at Sally for a moment, then reluctantly agreed. Sally had the feeling that although he grumbled, he wanted to please her and in the end would do anything she asked. This made her feel quite grown up and responsible. It also made her feel pity for Toby who seemed to need a guiding voice more than most.

They pushed junk they would never use to the back, and the things that were being used they organised into neat piles, with Toby instructed to brush and dust wherever there was dust to brush. Somehow, though, he seemed to touch things and then leave them much as they'd been before. He appeared busy but nothing much changed. Something was clearly on his mind when he stopped and asked, "Do you still believe in the beast?"

Sally looked at him shamefaced.

"No," she said. "There's no beast. I was wrong."

"Could be still down here," Toby suggested, swinging the little dustpan back and forth.

"Where?"

"Behind the walls, maybe. I dunno. Inside the building."

"No."

"I thought your stories came true."

"They don't."

"Don't they?"

"No."

Sally had tried hard not to think about the beast. The whole idea had appeared ridiculous weeks ago, and every time she remembered it she felt embarrassed. She'd known it at the time, of course, and so did the others, but everyone liked to believe in the impossible when the possible was so limited. She even wondered what the point of writing was altogether. Why make up stuff that was so obviously untrue and often silly? Why did she and her friends and almost all the children in the school listen so hard to made-up stories about people that didn't exist in places that didn't exist with things happening to them that never happened nor ever could happen? It was a mystery, even more so now that she saw how interesting life could be with a runaway boy hiding out in the belly of the school while everyone was running about above ground without a clue as to where he'd gone or why or how. So no, she didn't believe in the silly beast, and became annoyed with herself when, sometimes, in the dark and gloom of the hidden rooms, she imagined things that frightened her still.

"If there was a beast," she said to Toby, "you'd be a pile of bones on the floor by now, a scrumptious dinner for it."

"Do the other kids believe it? I bet they think the beast got me, don't they?"

"Some do. The dumb ones."

"Does Jonas believe it?"

"I don't know what he thinks. I don't even care what he thinks."

Toby became even more fond of his new friend. He did not like Jonas one bit, but he somehow felt that everyone else, especially the girls, did. It was reassuring to hear Sally say this. He decided he would tell her about the break-in and what he'd seen. He'd been afraid until now, but he really felt that Sally was on his side, and he'd never felt that before. She was talking though, and he didn't want to interrupt.

"Some think I could make the beast attack them

if they annoy me," she said. "It's weird."

"But you can't, can you?"

"No."

"And you don't believe in it no more?"

"Any more, Toby, any more. No."

"Why did you think it in the first place, then?" Sally didn't know. She told Toby that she'd thought she was special, but now she knew she wasn't.

"You're special to me," said Toby softly.

Sally stared at him as if he'd said the most unexpected thing anyone had ever said since the beginning of time. "You're here, aren't you?" he explained. "If you weren't special, you wouldn't be here, and you are here, the only one, so you must be special."

"Don't feel it," said Sally.

"Course you are. Sally?" She looked at him. He looked like he wanted to ask an important question, then asked it. "Do you think there's really beasts in the world? Real monsters?"

"Never seen one, so no."

"I do."

"No you don't. Have you ever seen one?"

"Maybe."

"That's not an answer. Yes or no?"

"In a way," he said.

"What way," asked Sally, sensing that he wanted to tell her something important.

He shook his head, not ready to spill any beans yet. He looked nervous, even afraid, but of what? There was nothing down here except foolish imaginings.

"I think you're brave," said Sally. "You didn't get scared down here all alone. That's brave. Didn't you think there was a real beast coming to get you?"

"Did at first. Just a bit. Then I got used to it. I don't scare too bad when I'm by meself."

"What scares you, Toby?"

"Nuffing," he lied, although it wasn't much of a lie. Not many things that scared others scared Toby Tinker and one of these things would have surprised anyone. What scared him most of all was that Sally might decide not to come back. She might get scared, or worse, fed up with his stupidity. But he couldn't tell her that, ever.

"Nothing at all?" asked Sally.

"No," he lied.

"Loads of things scare me," said Sally, "the worst thing at the moment is being wrong all the time. I was wrong about the beast and I'm wrong to come down here without telling."

"That's not wrong."

"Not to you, but it is to them," she pointed upstairs. "Can I tell you something?" she said.

"What?"

"You won't mind?"

"Might."

"It's a bit awkward."

Toby put on a puzzled look. What was she going to tell him? Would she say that she would never abandon him? Would she say how secretly clever he was? Would she say how much she liked this whole secret and that it would go on forever? Toby had no idea, but he thought it would be something good and kind and brilliant, like she was.

"You smell," she said.

Toby's face dropped. He didn't know whether to shout or laugh.

"I don't!"

"You do. You smell terrible. Better to tell you than keep it a secret."

Toby knew she was right, but he still got into a huff. He kicked away some invisible objects on the ground and started muttering to himself.

"So what," he said. "No one here."

"I'm here," said Sally, "unless you mean I'm no one?"

He didn't mean that, but he was too confused and agitated to think straight. They must have stood still for a long while, not speaking, until Sally said, "You've got to clean yourself up, Toby. If you don't, the police will smell you down here."

That made him laugh, but not a lot. He really thought she meant it.

"I can nip into the toilets, maybe," he said. "In the night."

"You'll have to wash everything," said Sally. "Even clothes."

"Can't you do them?" he asked.

"No! If I do, I'll get asked who they belong to. You have to do it."

"Bossy boots, that's what you are."

"It's for your own good, Toby. You can't pong

like that. It's not..."

Suddenly Toby put his finger to his lips and said, "Sshhh!"

"What...?"

"Sshhh! Listen!"

Sally listened. From somewhere up above came the distinct sounds of footsteps and voices.

Vacuum

They were dead quiet, listening, waiting..

"It's Mrs Parsons," whispered Sally, "and Mr Becker. What are they doing?"

"Ssshh!"

"Are they looking for the trapdoor?"

"Sshhh!"

The two teachers were making quite a bit of noise and were talking in loud enough voices to be heard.

"I'm sure they were left here a couple of years ago," said Mr Becker.

Lots of scrabbling around noises, then "Here they are! In this box. I knew it."

"Good. Let's take them up."

"There's some other stuff down here that might be useful. We must come down and tidy this place, you know. It's a pit. Who knows what we'll find?"

Sally whispered, "Toby, it's for the Christmas Play!"

"Sssh!"

"Did you hear something?" asked Mrs Parsons.

Apparently not, as the steps moved off and the voices faded.

"They were so close!" exclaimed Sally.

"What they doing there?" asked Toby.

"Looking for costumes and props," said Sally. "They were right on top of us!"

"They won't find me, will they?" asked Toby, full of anxiety.

Sally had to be honest and said yes, they might well find him, and tried again to persuade him to give himself up, but he wouldn't. Instead, she insisted that they dust the den and make plans to get it and Toby into shape.

"What we need," she said, "is a vacuum cleaner." Toby didn't know what that was. "A hoover, you know, an electric broom?" Toby nodded and asked why it was called a vacuum cleaner. "Because it's empty and sucks up rubbish, like your head," said Sally.

Toby watched her make his secret den liveable, but he didn't do much himself, mainly because he couldn't tell the difference between tidy and untidy. As long as he knew where things were, he was happy enough.

The next day, Sally brought him a face flannel, soap and a towel.

"I just don't know how you've survived down here so long," she said. "Really, Toby, you're like a skunk. You have to promise me you'll go to the bathroom tonight and use this stuff, get yourself clean and unsmelly. Here's a new shirt and a pair of my jeans."

"I can't put on girl's clothes," said Toby.

"It's not a fashion competition down here, Toby!" said Sally. "No one's going to laugh at you. And when they find you, which they will, at least you'll be shiny new."

Toby looked at her and hesitated before asking, "Why you doing this?"

"Doing what?" Sally said.

"Helping me," Toby said. "I mean, you're a clever clogs, you're good and nice and know everything. You never get into trouble and I never get out of it. What's in it for you?"

Sally took a moment to register this.

"What's in it for me? Are you joking?" He wasn't. "What do you think's in it for me, you idiot? A proper telling off, that's what. I must be nuts."

She looked hurt, but Toby wasn't sure how he'd hurt her.

When Sally came back the following day, Toby was indeed shiny new and almost sparkling. Sally's jeans and shirt fitted him quite well, and he looked like a different boy.

"That's better," Sally said. "I didn't mean what I said about the vacuum," she told him. "You're not really empty headed."

"And I didn't mean whatever I said to make you angry," said Toby.

They shook hands, which made them laugh, and Toby asked, quite surprisingly, "What you doing in school today?"

It was the first time he'd asked about lessons since Sally had found him.

"Usual. We've started a new topic. It's about the ancient Egyptians."

"They're great!" exclaimed Toby.

Sally nearly fell over with surprise.

"How do you know that?"

"I've seen pictures, init?" he answered. "They used to bury their kings in great big triangular things with loads of treasure."

"That's right," said Sally, "so they could have money when they were dead. Just in case they needed it. Teacher told us yesterday."

"But they wouldn't need it if they were dead, would they?" Toby asked.

"Well, they're all dead now," said Sally. "That's why they're called ancient. But their money is in museums so they couldn't have taken it with them."

For the next half hour, Sally told Toby all she'd learned about these ancient people who seemed once to have owned everything there was to own and now had vanished completely. They even had royal families with kings and queens.

"Like ours?" Toby asked.

"Yes, just like ours," said Sally.

Toby listened, fascinated. Now that he could read a little, in fact quite a lot, he half wished he was back in the class surrounded by books which might make a little more sense to him now.

"There was a Toot something," said Sally, "who was buried for ages when they found him. He had loads of treasure with him."

"So he didn't use it?"

"No, it was still there. Billions of pounds of it. Really nice stuff, masks and things. All gold. You'd love it. They said it was really lucky to find it all because usually all the graves were robbed. I bet if you were alive then, that's just what you'd do," said Sally.

Toby laughed and said why not, but Sally gave him a scolding look and Toby started to see a little light at the end of his pilfering tunnel.

"Don't know why we have to do all that stuff," said Toby. "I mean, the pictures are nice, but it's all rubbish, init, all dead and gone now."

"We have to do them," said Sally. "Mr Jarvis said they're on the National Curricular."

Toby asked her what else they'd done in school and he did his best to listen. Sally had a way of making things interesting, things that a few weeks before Toby would have thought were rubbish. He still did, to a certain extent, but not so much. He began to see that he could fill his vacuum of a head with different things, better things, and somehow he sensed that it might make him a different and better boy. Sally left him her book on the Egyptians, telling Toby that she'd make up an excuse to Mr Jarvis.

"That's bad," said Toby.

"Not half as bad as all this," said Sally, gesturing to the den.

She told him to try writing a little about the things she'd taught him. For practise.

"Just an idea," she said. "Got to go now, Toblerone. Ready?"

"That's not my name. And no, I ain't ready."

"Going anyway."

"Go on then."

Toby tried to sound careless, but he was increasingly upset when Sally left him.

"I hate thinking of you all alone down here," said Sally.

"I'm alright."

"See you later, Toblerone."

"Alright. Go on. Be careful."

"I will."

And she was.

Confession

One morning, Mr Jarvis asked to speak with Sally. He told her that the police had asked to see her story and he'd sent them a copy. Now he handed her a sealed letter.

"Will you take this home with you, Sally?" he asked. "It's for your mother and father."

Sally blanched.

"Am I in trouble, sir?"

"I don't know Sally, are you? I hope not, but I want to talk with your parents about a few things."

Sally didn't know what to say. She couldn't tell lies easily. Perhaps this was a good thing, she wasn't sure.

"Take it with you tonight," Mr Jarvis said. "You won't forget?"

"No, sir."

"Good. You're okay, are you, Sally?"

"There's nothing wrong with me, sir. I'm fine."

"Then there's nothing to worry about, is there?"

A thought passed through Sally's mind which made her feel terribly ashamed. She wondered what would happen if she didn't give the letter to her parents, but she knew straight away it would be a disastrous decision; she'd be found out and all hell would break loose.

She gave the letter to her mother, full of apprehensions, and rightly so. She felt that the world was catching up with her lies and closing in, ever so slowly but ever so surely.

"He wants to talk with us," her mother said. "I'll go in tomorrow."

"You don't have to," said Sally, hopefully. "I'm alright, really I am. You can write him a letter. I'll take it."

"No, I don't mind. I'm sure he wouldn't call us for nothing. Sal, is there anything you need to tell me?"

"No, mum."

"You're sure you're not in trouble?"

"No. He said I wasn't."

"Perhaps I can come with you early to Book Club tomorrow. That will save interrupting lessons."

"No!" exclaimed Sally, and then, "no," in a lighter voice, hiding her panic. "Book Club is closed tomorrow."

"Alright, I'll come around lunch time. You'll tell him, will you?"

"Yes, mum."

But first, that evening, she told Toby.

"Did you read it?" he asked.

"No, of course I didn't."

"I would have done."

"I bet you would. Do you think they know anything?"

"If they did, they would have posted the letter or phoned your home. It's nothing."

"I'm worried Toby. I'm getting horrible feelings in my tummy. Grown-ups are not stupid, you know. They can work things out. I was thinking, I might not be able to come every day anymore."

"Why?"

There was a look of alarm on Toby's face just as there was a look of anxiety on Sally's. She'd been making up stories for weeks, only these weren't ones you put down on paper and read to the class and pretended were true, these were lies that twisted the truth and upset the apple cart. And yet, Sally felt that a little touch of goodness was on her side here and that was confusing. On one hand she knew she was doing wrong, but on the other she felt that, if everyone who loved her understood, they would give her a hug and say everything was forgiven. She told Toby how many questions she'd been asked and how often she'd had to hide what was going on, over and over.

"Grown-ups ask you loads of questions all the time," said Toby. "You just stand there and listen till they're finished and then that's it. Nothing happens."

"But I've been lying to my mum and dad!" said Sally, exasperated that Toby still had no idea of how she felt. "They'll be furious and hurt."

Toby really didn't understand. He tried, but the idea of grown-ups being upset was beyond him. He had a vague notion of some kind of law and order that made things tick, but it was too vague too worry about.

"I don't want people to know yet," said Toby. "I just like you as my teacher. I don't want no one else."

"No*body* else," said Sally the Teacher, "but they'll find out, Toby. They probably know something already."

"Don't say nuffing," said Toby. "They can't make you talk."

Sally thought differently, that 'they' definitely could make her talk, or that, in the end, she'd tell them everything willingly. She had to. Toby wasn't going to live in the dark and dismal den forever, was he? But she had to admit, it was special. She didn't want to give him up. She'd come to feel sympathy for him. She could see how hard he wanted to read and write like everyone else. She couldn't understand how his funny brain worked, but she knew that he wasn't a bad boy. In fact, she sensed he was a very good hearted boy. If things were wrong with him, they could still be put right.

"Oh, Toby, you just don't understand, do you. It's worse than ever out there. You're on the news every day. You're in the papers. Everyone is worried sick about you. And I'm the only one who knows you're alright. Can't you see that's a difficult secret?"

Toby said, reluctantly, "Maybe."

"No, not maybe. Definitely."

"I'll tell you a secret too, though."

"What?"

"This is the best time I've had in my life," said Toby, "and you're the best friend I've had in my life, too. Nobody ever did anyfing as kind as what you've done. I don't want it to stop and go back to normal. I hate normal."

"Oh, Toby!"

The two children sat sad and silently for a while, puzzling out the grown-up web of words.

"I'll tell you anuver secret," said Toby. "I've been meaning to say this for days, but I didn't."

"What secret?"

"About the break-in."

Sally had forgotten the break-in completely. It had been the talk of the moment, but then Toby had disappeared and no one spoke about it any more. The hole in the fence had been repaired, the money replaced and that was that.

"I saw who did it," said Toby. "I saw them doing it. The fing is," and he hesitated, "they saw me, too."

"Who did, Toby?"

Toby couldn't say the word easily.

"Jason."

For a moment, Sally didn't know who he meant, then it all clicked.

Jason Stamp was Jonas Stamp's brother. Five years older and five times badder. He'd already been in trouble with the police, and everyone knew he was a rotten egg. But Sally saw what was bothering Toby. Right away, without him saying any more. She put her hand on his shoulder and said, "Oh Toby, you poor thing."

They'd seen him, and once the Stamps felt threatened, they were double the menace. Triple. Toby hadn't wanted to wait around and see what they would do. He knew what they would do. Only an idiot would wait for the Stamps to put the fear of God into you or worse, do you damage. They would, Sally knew it, everyone knew it. They were a hard family who would bash you as soon as look at you.

"I ain't scared," said Toby, who was scared to death, in fact.

"I know you're not!" said Sally and she gave him the kind of hug she used to give her teddy bear when she was five years old.

"It's just that they're... you know, and I didn't fancy getting hurt. So what with your beast and stuff, I saw this place and thought I'd hide out. It was kind of strange really, as they made the hole in the fence that let me in. I thought that was funny in a funny peculiar way," he said.

Sally wasn't laughing, and neither was Toby, even though he smiled ruefully.

"You're a brave boy," said Sally. "You have to deal with so much and you do it all by yourself in your own way. I think you're fantastic."

Toby thought the same about Sally, but decided that he better not say it because she might think it sounded silly. Or worse, lovey dovey. He'd been almost as afraid of owning up about what happened as he had of what the Stamps would do to him if they found him. The fear had hounded him every day since he'd seen them cutting the fence wire and them seeing him seeing them. He'd hid for a while, but where could he hide forever? Where would be the last place they'd look? Well, he'd found it and they hadn't. He'd been safe for weeks and they'd never ever get to him.

Sally's beast came back to haunt her, but not in the way she imagined. It was still there, but had changed. It was the beast of bullying and fear, of strong people hurting weak people, of monsters with two legs and two arms but no brain. Her silly creature seemed even sillier compared to this real nastiness in the world. She wanted to hug Toby till all the fear left him. She wanted to hug all his troubles away and let him be free to grow without being warped by thieves and louts and all kinds of cruelties.

Toby told her what had happened, what he'd seen and how he knew from their looks that they had him marked. He also knew that clever Sally Shakespeare understood everything he was feeling even without him telling her, which embarrassed him, so he perked up, changed the subject and said, "Do you want to see what I've did?"

"'Done'", muttered Sally. "Alright."

Toby dug around in a cardboard box he'd found and took out an exercise book. It was filled with writing, twenty pages of letter after letter, sound after sound.

"Toby!" said Sally, trying to rouse herself from the overwhelming sense of injustice. "That's amazing! You've worked so hard."

"I just learned them words like you said," he told her. "I read what you wrote, then I closed my eyes and spelled them in my head, then I wrote them down ten times each."

Whatever method he was using, he was definitely getting the hang of writing and spelling.

"Am I good?" he asked her.

"The best," said Sally. "I'll give you a star," and she drew a picture of a star in his book.

Toby had never had a star, not for anything. It had never occurred to him that he would ever get one. Stars and Toby didn't go together. They were like oil and water, they didn't mix. But here was a solid gold star at the end of all his efforts given to him by the cleverest girl in the whole wide world. He was more proud of that star than anything else he'd ever done, although he had to admit, he hadn't done much, not yet. But he would; he told himself he would.

Writer

Over the next week he practised handwriting for hours, going over and over patterns Sally had shown him until he got them just right. He mastered the alphabet, capitals and lower case, and started on punctuation marks which had always puzzled him. He also did sums, troubling his brain with place value and the four rules as if they were the hardest things anyone had ever invented. When he grew restless, he would look at the books Sally had brought him and found himself reading whole sentences, even from the harder books.

'This ain't so hard' he said to himself.

His eyes hurt because he was straining to read in the dim lantern light, but he kept going, deciding that he would probably spend the rest of his life there. It was nice to have a friend and there was nothing outside that he missed, except his gran, and she was outside The Outside, so that didn't count.

At night, he would explore the school and sneak

into the playground by opening a window. It was a mysterious place in the dark, very different to the way it was during the day. Silence surrounded the building like a cloak of invisibility from a famous story Sally had told him about. He saw everything, but no one could see him. He imagined what people would say when, or perhaps only if, they discovered that he was alive, and not just alive but clever and smart like the rest of them. He wasn't such a dodo after all.

It was Toby who had the bright idea to open a window so that Sally could get into school at any time. He told her which one it was and she climbed in, feeling like a thief in the night, but not stealing anything, so she wasn't a proper thief. If the school gate was locked, Sally used the 'door' in the wire fence she and the others had made weeks before. It seemed like years before, actually, but it wasn't. Time was all messed up. The only thing that could go wrong was the hall door being locked, but it never was. The schoolkeeper didn't think that anyone would be able to get through the fence and into the school building. And why would they want to? It wasn't Fort Knox. There was no gold or hidden treasures in the building. Kids did their best to get away from school, he thought, so why would they want to creep inside?

A month passed, a whole month. Sally visited whenever she could, amazed that she was getting away with it. But the secrecy and the strain took its toll, and one day she turned up with red eyes. Her parents had spoken to Mr Jarvis quite a few times, and to the headmaster. They all knew something was wrong but they didn't know what it was. Sally had been within a whisker of telling them, but she didn't say a thing. Seeing her upset, Toby wasn't sure what to say or do.

"It'll be alright," he said with a kind of worldly wisdom. "Fings always are in the end. My gran told me that. She was okay, my gran was, until she died. Then she wasn't."

Toby looked again at the locket with the picture of his grandmother.

"Did she die a long time ago?" Sally asked, trying to cheer herself up by talking about Toby's troubles instead.

"Last year. She'd tell me not to worry about things. She said that everything turns out all white in the end."

"It's 'alright', Toby, not 'all white'"

"Is it? Well, same fing. She was clever, my gran."

"She cared about you, didn't she?"

"Suppose so."

"Everyone has someone to care about. Don't you think so, Toby?"

"I don't. I'm going to stay by meself. Best way."

"What about me, Toby? Don't you care about me?"

Toby shrugged and looked embarrassed.

"You gonna teach me anything today?" he asked.

Sally answered glumly, "If you like."

"Don't sound like you do."

"I'm worried, Toby. Don't you understand?"

"About what?"

"I've just told you! Don't you care what happens to me?"

"They're only going to shout at you," he said. "They're not going to hit you or anyfing."

"Toby, you're so selfish!" Sally lost her cool for a moment. "I don't know why I helped you at all. All you do is think of yourself. You don't care what happens to me at all."

"I do."

"If you did you'd be more sympathetic."

"I dunno what that means."

Sally almost laughed in desperation.

"It means seeing things the way others see them, and feeling the way they do so you can help them."

"Oh. How do you do that, then? I don't know how you feel, do I?"

"You have to use your imagination, Toby, and don't tell me you don't know what that is. Anyway, you shouldn't even have to try. If you can't do it, you can't do it and that's that."

"Can't you teach me?"

"Don't be silly. Of course I can't teach you."

Toby thought for a few moments and then said, "I suppose if my gran had shouted at me, I'd be upset."

"That's right, you would," said Sally, "but it isn't only being shouted at, it's all the lies I've told. I feel so bad about them."

"Lies don't do no harm."

"Who says? I think they do. They do to me. And I'm the one that's telling them."

"You make me feel like it's my fault."

"Well it is, isn't it?"

Now it was Toby's turn to be downcast. He felt like he couldn't do right in this world at all. Even down in this lonely place, away from almost everyone else, he'd upset the one person who'd found him and helped him. Not purposely, but just by being what he was.

"Sorry," he said.

Sally rubbed her eyes dry and looked up. What she saw upset her. Tears were running down Toby's cheeks.

"Oh, Toby," she said, "I'm sorry, too. How are we going to get out of this mess?"

"Gawd knows."

And when he said this, they both started laughing, softly at first, but then louder. Sally repeated his words, "Gawd knows!" and they laughed louder, at the same time trying to control themselves in case anyone heard. If it died down a little Toby repeated the magic words and the hysterics doubled. Sally said them too, making it all impossible to bear. They lay on the floor and rolled over, holding their sides whispering 'Gawd knows!" for about five minutes. In this way they got rid of much of their anger, if not their anxiety.

When eventually they calmed down they were both tired.

"That was fun," said Toby. "I ain't laughed like that for ages."

"I haven't laughed like that for ages," corrected Sally. "Neither have I," at which point, they started again.

"Do you fink we're drunk?" asked Toby.

"We haven't been drinking, have we?" replied Sally. "Unless there's something in these fizzy drinks."

"Perhaps we're both mad," suggested Toby, "from being locked up."

"I'm not locked up," said Sally. "I can go whenever I want."

"Then I'm mad and you've caught it."

"Can you catch madness?"

"Dunno. Why not?"

"People will say we were mad to do this. That's exactly what they'll say. They'll say I was mad to do it and you were mad to help me. Everyone'll say it and everyone can't be wrong. Isn't that right?"

But when she looked at him, Sally started laughing for the umpteenth time and that set him off and another crazy five minutes passed.

"I think I've wet myself," said Toby.

"Oh, no," said Sally, who at the thought of Toby wetting himself burst out into giggles yet again.

"I have," said Toby. "What am I going to do? I'm like a baby."

"Yes you are. Baby Toby. What you'll have to do is wash all your things and hang them up."

Sally suddenly saw how vulnerable he was and

how much he depended on her. She felt so sorry for him, and at the same time was angry with him. He was a confused boy and he had confused her. There he was, all wet and ashamed, not knowing what to do. She told him to make sure he cleaned up when she was gone and to use the clean clothes she'd brought. Next time, she'd take the dirty ones away and wash them, in secret. Everything was in secret now.

"Will you be alright ?" she asked.

"Yeh, yeh, go on. Quicker you go the quicker I can clean up."

Toby's predicament had taken away his softer side and made him brusque and seemingly rude again, but Sally understood why and left without an argument.

"See you."

"See you."

She left him behind, her heart in shreds at Toby's predicament, not knowing what to do for the best, but ready, peculiarly enough, and for no reason she could understand, to laugh all over again, only this time her eyes were watering with tears of confusion as well as humour.

XYZ

When she arrived home one evening after a flying visit to Toby, her mother cast her an inquisitive look and said, "Sally. My Sally."

"Yes, mum?"

"You look... different."

When she looked in the mirror in her room, she had to agree, she'd changed. There was something in her eyes that was different to the Sally she remembered. She went to bed thinking about how she was changing and preparing herself for the trouble that was sure to fall on her like a ton of bricks. Inexplicably though, she was less afraid than she'd have thought. She didn't like the idea of being found out, but she'd only done, every tiny step of the way, what she'd thought was right, and that was what her parents and teachers had taught her to do, so they wouldn't be too angry, surely?

The days often felt long and difficult. Her parents had spoken to the headmaster a few times over the past weeks and they all knew something was bothering her. It was a burden, carrying this secret around like a ball and chain. Amazingly, her parents hadn't discovered that the Book Club was a lie. The word 'lie' sent tremors down Sally's spine. What would she answer if she was found out? Would she tell the truth and betray Toby? What else could she do? She could do, she thought, what Toby had suggested and say nothing. Just be quiet. She would never be trusted again. Anything that she said, any favour she asked, any word she gave, she would never be fully believed, never in her whole life. The fear made her tremble. Her love and happiness at home was based on trust between her and her parents. Now she was about to lose it all. They would look on her with doubt and life would never be the same.

"I wish I'd never written that stupid story," she said to herself. But there was no point regretting. She'd written it and that was that.

And what would her friends say?

Once the secret was out they would distrust her and dislike her. How could they do anything else? Friends are for confiding in and helping, not for lying to and keeping secrets from. Michelle and Jackie would disown her. They wouldn't want a friend who didn't tell them everything, not one who could keep such a secret. Like her parents, they would never trust her again. Neither would Mr Jarvis, a teacher who had been so kind to her and so enthusiastic about her work. What would he think? Naturally he would think like everyone else. He would resent her lies and deceit in hiding the truth from everyone who had been concerned about Toby. He would look at her in class in a different way. He might not even look at her at all, except with anger because of her lies.

It was a Friday, the end of another week at school and the end of another week of teaching Toby the 'Three Rs'. Sally planned to sneak back that evening but her aunt and uncle were coming and she had to stay home. Normally, Sally had time to herself, but this weekend was fully taken up with family duties. Not one second did she stop thinking about Toby, alone in the gloom, probably believing that she'd abandoned him. She would never do that, of course she wouldn't, but he'd still think it, and he'd lock the window out of anger. He would cut off his nose to spite his face, would Toby. He was like that, but a lot of people might do the same, in his position.

Sally racked her brains to get away, but she was kept busy all Saturday and all Sunday. She felt dreadful. In all the weeks she'd known Toby was skulking in the belly of the school, she'd never missed two days in a row; rarely even one.

They were having a late Sunday lunch when the phone rang. Sally's mother glanced at her husband and he glanced at Sally, both with puzzled, almost distraught expressions. Sally looked at them in turn as casually as she could, sure that her thoughts were leaking out onto the Sunday roast. Sally's mother was as white as a ghost. She wouldn't tell Sally who the call was from, and all kinds of ideas went through Sally's mind.

Sally felt sure they were closing in, finding her

out, knowing what a liar she was, and what a bad girl. She hated herself sometimes, but didn't know what to do for the best. Then she thought of Toby and knew that he came first. He was alive and well and that was what counted.

It was late Sunday afternoon before she had, at last, a little time to herself. When she told her mother she was off to see Michelle, she was puzzled by her mother's answer.

"Be careful, Sal," her mother whispered. "You know dad and I love you. Whatever happens."

Sally stared at her mother, once again seeing grown ups say so much more than was hidden in a few words. She almost ran out of the house, feeling an invisible net tightening around her but deciding this was just fear, and she had to conquer her fears, for Toby's sake.

She was no more than a hundred yards down the road when her mother, back home, picked up the telephone, fighting back tears, calling the number she'd been given days before.

Sally reached the school quickly and in her hurry didn't check around as carefully as usual. If she had, she might have seen the white car parked some way away where two people, a man and a woman, sat very still, watching and waiting. It would have been too far, even if she had noticed them, to see the woman pick up a phone and whisper into it.

Thank goodness, the window was open! Well done Toby! He hadn't locked it out of anger after all. It had been open ever since Toby had thought of this new way in. She'd climbed in and out a dozen times since, closing it after her, checking to make sure no one had seen her, then heading towards the hall, the stairs down, the network of rooms and the trapdoor. It was exciting every time, like a TV programme. She felt clever, doing something no one else in the world knew about, except Toby of course. The secret made them both powerful, in charge of their lives, not being told what to do by anyone but doing it themselves, and for a good reason. That was important, and Sally kept telling herself this despite the doubts and the guilt. This was for a good reason. Toby was a damaged little boy. No one cared about him and she herself had hurt him. But she saw him differently now, she'd seen him differently for weeks, a sad and bothered boy doing his best to understand what everyone else seemed to understand so easily. That spurred her on, gave her courage when the doubts got the better of her.

She rapped on the trapdoor and it opened almost at once.

Toby's face was streaming with tears. His eyes were red and blotchy and he bore a look of unutterable sadness.

"Toby, what's wrong?"

"You!"

Sally knew what he would say but he could hardly get the words out, he was so agitated.

"You never came and you never came and you never came!"

Sally saw that her absence was a frustration to

her but to Toby it was the end of the world. He looked devastated, as if she'd done it on purpose.

"I couldn't help it, Toby. You know that!"

"I fought you weren't coming no more."

Sally didn't know what to say. She'd done everything she could to see Toby every day, but the past couple of days had been impossible. He had to understand that! But clearly, he didn't. Sally understood how the world appeared different, even if the same thing was happening. People saw with their own eyes in their own way. Toby was wretched. He thought his best friend had deserted him. It didn't make any difference that Sally had no way to let him know what was going on; she hadn't turned up and there was no excuse. She tried to excuse herself but he wouldn't listen.

She switched to teacher mode.

"Stop talking like that, Toby! You say I 'thought', not I 'fought', and you knew I would come again, you knew! I've been here every day for weeks. You don't have to cry."

There was nothing to do but wait. Eventually Toby's tears dried up. He wiped his eyes with his sleeves and seemed to pull himself together.

"Here," she said. "I brought some tissues."

Toby took one. He blew his nose and threw the tissue on the floor.

"Toby!"

He picked it up and put it into a dustbin made from an old cardboard box.

"What happened?" he asked, snivelling and

snorting away his tears. Sally told him that her parents had kept her busy and this was the first chance she'd had to get away. To Toby, this was very hard to imagine. His parents never did anything with him and all his time was his own, so naturally he thought it was the same for everyone, just as Sally found it hard to imagine that level of neglect.

Feeling that Toby was quietening down a little, Sally glanced around and saw immediately how busy he must have been.

"You've washed all your clothes," she said, "and hung them up!"

Toby had made a washing line from some plastic piping which he'd laid horizontally over two wooden crates.

"I cleaned meself too," he whispered, wiping a drop of water from his nose. "I went to the kitchen and washed in the sink."

"Really," Sally almost laughed. "Did you stand in it?"

"Yeh. It was alright. There was even hot water."

"Didn't you make a mess?"

"A bit. But I tidied up. S'alright, miss."

He still called her miss, sometimes. She didn't know what to make of him, even now. She told him to call her Sally, but she was like mother and teacher rolled into one, and he found it hard to think of her as the same clever clogs Sally he'd known in class.

Toby was remarkably clean, considering he'd been hiding in the dusty underbelly of a school for weeks, but there were tear lines down each cheek.

He was wearing some of the clothes she'd brought him. He had on a pair of her jeans and one of her pullovers, a bottle green one knitted by Sally's mother. The jeans were a nice fit but the pullover was too big so he'd rolled up the sleeves. He also had on a pair of red socks which hung loosely around his toes. Sally thought he looked more like a teddy bear than ever.

Books were spread around as if he'd been studying all the time for some important examination. His eyes were red, and not just from crying. He really had been working hard, letter by letter, from ABC to XYZ, struggling over sounds and meanings, and all manner of sums, determined to get his brain into shape. There were scribblings on countless pieces of paper, books with bookmarks and broken pencils, all testimony to his efforts.

"I'll make you a cup of tea," he whispered, wiping away the last of the tears.

He took out the stove and skilfully set it up, filling a saucepan from a plastic container then lighting the gas and waiting for the water to boil. They watched it heat up in silence until Sally said, "I'm sorry, Toby. I didn't mean to make you cry."

"Thas alright. You didn't do nuffing on purpose."

When the water boiled, he put tea bags into two mugs, pilfered from the kitchen, and started to pour, but his hand was shaking and he spilt some, so Sally took the pan and poured the boiling water instead.

"I ain't got no milk."

"No probs," said Sally. "I don't mind tasteless black tea in dirty cups."

They sipped the hot excuse for tea silently until Toby felt a little like his old self. He said, "I been really busy. I was in the kitchen for hours. I washed everything. I washed me. I did all my clothes. I cleaned up. I thought you'd be pleased."

"I am. It's really good, Toby."

"I also did a load of work. Look."

Sally was impressed and touched. There were reams of work, even proper sentences starting with capital letters and ending with full stops.

"I been writing a diary," said Toby.

"Is it private?" asked Sally.

Toby shrugged, then handed over an exercise book to Sally who started to read the first entry and then stopped.

"It's bad, init?" he asked.

"No, it's fine," said Sally. "I just don't understand how you can get so good so quickly. Are you sure you want me to read it, Toby? Diaries are private things and only you should read them. Unless you've been dead a long time when anyone can."

"But I don't want to be dead a long time. What's the good of anyone reading it if I've been dead a long time? That's daft. You can read it. I don't mind. Go on."

Sally read:

Been hear nerely too weaks. Bean out nites sumtimes but dont care if i dont. Got used to it. Dun me washing and evrything. Tydied up for sally shakspear. Sally is my new frend. She comes down to giv me fings and talk. She ain't given me away which i dont no why she ain't. She will get into truble. This is the furst time ive wrote fings in order like this. I hope i get better becoz if i dont sally sez ill be stoopid for evr. She told me abowt kapitl letrs and fool stops and stuff. My spelling is bad but i can spel bettr than befor which shows how useless school is. Sally (capital letters died at this point) *dident come today but i fink she will come tomorow she sed she mite not be abel to come evryday.*

next day. forgot wich day it is. sally dident come agen i hope she aint forgot. she woodent forget i dont think but she mite be skaird or sumthink like that. but she sed she wood and she ain't so she betr soon. i will leeve the window open like it woz today in case she comes tomorow. i dont like it az much by myself az i did. its mor fun when sally is here and she iz a gud techr. i hope she dont mind my speling.

i went into the hall and did the ropes agen. i dident get all the apratuz out but i klimed the ropes and tuchd the seeling. i went up the bars and over the top and down but in a way it ain't az much fun az when kids are doing it wiv you.

i think i will come out from hear soon. i cood stay if i wanted but i think i will come out.

i will rite this dairy evry day from now on.

my name is Toby Tinker. full stop.

"Do you think you will?" asked Sally.

"What?"

"Write your diary every day from now on?"

"Might."

"I understood everything, Toby. I mean the spelling is still terrible, but I understood everything. Here, give me a pencil. I'll make corrections of all the words you got wrong. Not all, but most."

Sally spent a few minutes writing out the misspelled words correctly.

"I really fought you weren't going to come today. I fought you'd got into trouble or was afraid."

"No, I wasn't in trouble. Not yet. But I will be."

"I fought you'd told someone about me."

"I haven't, though. No one."

Toby considered this. He'd never had much faith in other people but Sally had never let him down, not on purpose, at least. He watched her correcting his hopeless work, like a proper teacher, just for him. He didn't want to disturb her, there were so many mistakes, every single word, almost, but she didn't grumble and she didn't tell him off.

When she'd finished, she put the pencil down and sat back.

He said, "I don't like it as much as I did at first down here. I was thinking that I might come out soon."

"I wish you would."

"It's still nice though, having somewhere nobody knows about. Don't you like it?"

In a way, she did. It was a good secret because she was doing something good, but also a bad secret because so many people were distressed about Toby. They really were, not because they knew him and cared for him, but because everyone feared the idea of something horrible happening to him or to any child. It was the worst thing in the world.

"And I ain't seen the beast here. Not once."

"That's because there isn't one."

"It might be somewhere else."

"I don't think so," said Sally. "It's a baby idea."

"Grown-ups think of them too," said Toby. "They write books about them, I've seen them in shops. But yours is better."

"I won't ever write about a beast again."

"You should, though. You could make millions of pounds. You'd never have to work."

"Do you think so?"

"Yes."

"Well, maybe when I'm grown up and I understand everything better I'll change my mind."

"I reckon the beast still might be real."

"Toby, why don't you leave off about the beast?"

"Cos I'm interested. I thought your story was great."

"Didn't do any good, though, did it? Got you into trouble. Got me into trouble. Got Joanna a broken foot. It's made a mess of things Toby. A big one."

Toby disagreed. He'd learned more in the past few weeks than he had in ten years of being a foolish, lonely little boy. He'd learned how to read and write and do sums, which was important, but he'd also learned that people could like him. If Sally Shakespeare liked him, then others might too, despite him still being a bit thick. He wasn't sure that she'd stay friends with him once they got out of the Dismal Den into the world again, but she might, and even if she didn't, he'd always remember these days with her. No one could take that away.

"You know what we should do?" he said.

"What?"

"We should write something on the wall to say we were here."

"'Writing on the wall'?" Sally repeated quietly. "There's a saying like that. It means you're close to the end."

"The end of what, miss?"

"Of anything. And there's nothing you can do about it."

Toby took a knife and started carving something on the back wall.

"What are you going to write?" asked Sally.

"Writing my name."

He read out the words he was carving:

"'Toby Tinker was here.' Now you do yours."

Sally stood up and carved, 'and so was Sally Shakespeare'.

"I should put the date," said Sally. She added it, then Toby took the knife and underneath it he carved the word, 'hearows'.

"Is that how you spell it?" he asked.

"No," said Sally, "but people will understand."

They stepped back to admire the carving.

"Do you think anyone will ever read it?" asked Toby.

"They might."

"Wonder what they'll think. They might not come for hundreds of years. Maybe thousands of years."

"The school won't stand up for that long."

"Good. Hope it falls down tomorrow."

"Then no one will see what we've written."

"Good again," said Toby. "Don't want every Tom, Dick and Harry nosing around. It's a secret, init, just between you and me. Whenever grown-ups tell us off we can remember it and know that we know something they don't know."

"Will that make us feel better?"

"Course it will. I'll remember you coming to look after me and not telling no one and doing all the fings you did."

The carving was special. It was like sending a text that could never be erased. Cast in stone, that's what it was. There was no Delete button, either. The only way their names were ever going to vanish from the wall was when the Earth itself swallowed the school. And even then, the rock would last and bits of their names would fall into eternity. Maybe when the Earth died, billions of years in the future, their names would be hurled into space on a vast journey for another few billion years until some alien race on a distant world found it and saw that Toby Tinker and Sally Shakespeare had been somewhere, sometime.

"Wassat!" exclaimed Toby.

A sound, some kind of movement, behind them. They turned.

The trapdoor flipped open with a thump and a light appeared in the darkness beyond. Both children caught their breath for they believed, despite everything, that at last the beast had come for them.

And in a way it had.

THE END

Discussion Points

- Did Sally's story come true?

- Why was Toby Tinker so angry?

- How did Toby hide his frustration?

- What did you think of Sally's friends?

- Did Sally do the right thing?

- What would you have done?

- What did you think of the adults in the story?

- What was Toby's problem?

- Describe the relationship between the two children.

- What would have happened if any of the other children in the story had found him?

- What other ways could Sally have used to help Toby?

- What would have happened if Sally had told on him straight away?

- Who discovered them?

- How were they eventually found out?

- What happens after the story ends?

The Cover

The wonderful cover of this book was designed by a final year student in the Illustration Course at the University of Lincoln. We ran a competition which many of the students entered. Of course, only one could win, but I thought it would be a pity for readers not to see the other entries, they are all so good. Here they are:

Sarah Hughes	Christina Billett	Sarah Crosby	Stuart Herrington
Grace Sandford	Stephen Sharpe	Emma Keller	Joanne Cooper
Helen Witt	Rachel Sanson	Sophie Brown	Hayley Wells

Cosmo	Pip Keech	Jessica Wickham	Emma Ferry
Heather Burns	Ashley Tunbridge	James Hughes	Kathryn Knight

These black and white images are just to give a flavour of the covers created by the university students here in Lincoln. You can see the covers in glorious colour at the Hawkwood website, www.hawkwoodbooks.co.uk. It was anything but easy to select a 'winner' and, as we discussed, winning can be something of an illusion. A decision was made based on style, relevance and originality. I wish I could print twenty versions of the book, each with a different cover.

I hope you admire the winning entry, and indeed all the entries, as much as we do.

Hawkwood Books

Lincoln 2013

Hawkwood Books

Thank you for reading this story; I hope you enjoyed it. We have other unusual, entertaining and thoughtful titles. Here are some of them:

For similar ages:

Star Games
The Secret
Dinosaur Boy
The Last Garden
A Boy Arrives
The Fantastic Galactic Construction Kit
The Fantastic Prismatic Construction Kit

For young adults:

Train Ghost
Miracle Girl
Cool World

And for younger readers

Byte, The Computer Mite
Piccadilly Mitzie

For more information visit:
www.hawkwoodbooks.co.uk